Praise for *That Night*

A Finalist for the PEN/Faulkner Award and the Los Angeles Times Book Prize

"A slim novel of almost nineteenth-century richness, a novel that celebrates the life of its suburban world at the same moment that it mourns that world's failures and disappointments . . . In spite of its brevity, *That Night* is a wonderfully unfettered, ample novel, one that celebrates voice, personality and feeling when so much fiction avoids those rewarding characteristics . . . Splendid."
—David Leavitt, *The New York Times Book Review*

"In *That Night* McDermott lovingly bares the suburban soul—no, she bares the American soul—hidden behind metal Venetian blinds and crisply manicured hedges. In the end we glimpse her characters—the lovers and the child narrator—all grown and transformed by one summer night."   —Alice Leccese Powers, NPR

"McDermott has gracefully captured the haunted essence of suburban fence-culture—that eclipsed decade when you may have dared a glance at the sun, and wound up paying for it the rest of your life."   —Gail Caldwell, *The Boston Globe*

"A strong, eloquent novel . . . McDermott writes clean, simple prose that serves her story beautifully. This novel is as carefully constructed as a poem, giving off a lustrous glow, and is poignant in the telling."   —*People*

"McDermott is so assured, her prose so spare and swift, that not once does she come even close to sentimentality. With tremendous skill and control, she counters the poignancy of the past with sharp realities."   —*The Plain Dealer* (Cleveland)

"McDermott brilliantly manipulates the particulars of this story, these characters, and that night to show them as both unique and universal . . . Perfectly evokes the suburban climate of the sixties."
—*San Francisco Chronicle*

"Evokes in a masterly way the one moment when a single incident so thoroughly assaults the sensibilities as to alter life significantly . . . McDermott seamlessly employs several innovative techniques that would have stymied a less intrepid writer."
—*The Baltimore Sun*

"Constructed as tightly as a rose . . . McDermott writes of the poignancy of Then and Now with a grace and richness admirably unmuffled by the fashionable tendency to 'minimalize' emotion."
—Rosellen Brown, *Ms.*

ALICE McDERMOTT

That Night

Alice McDermott is the author of eight novels, including *The Ninth Hour*; *Someone*; *After This*; *Charming Billy*, winner of the 1998 National Book Award; *At Weddings and Wakes*; and *That Night*—all published by FSG. *That Night*, *At Weddings and Wakes*, and *After This* were finalists for the Pulitzer Prize. She is also the author of the essay collection *What About the Baby? Some Thoughts on the Art of Fiction*. Her stories and essays have appeared in *The New York Times*, *The Washington Post*, *The New Yorker*, *Harper's Magazine*, and other publications. For more than two decades she was the Richard A. Macksey Professor for Distinguished Teaching in the Humanities at Johns Hopkins University and a member of the faculty at the Sewanee Writers' Conference. McDermott lives with her family outside Washington, D.C.

Also by
Alice McDermott

That Night

That Night

a novel

ALICE McDERMOTT

Picador
Farrar, Straus and Giroux
New York

Picador
120 Broadway, New York 10271

Copyright © 1987 by Alice McDermott
All rights reserved
Printed in the United States of America
Originally published in 1987 by Farrar, Straus and Giroux
First paperback edition, 2012
Paperback reissue edition, 2023

Library of Congress Cataloging-in-Publication Data
Names: McDermott, Alice, author.
Title: That night : a novel / Alice McDermott.
Description: Paperback reissue edition. | New York : Picador ; Farrar, Straus
    and Giroux, 2023.
Identifiers: LCCN 2022043524 | ISBN 9781250881373 (paperback)
Subjects: LCSH: Love in adolescence—Fiction. | At-risk youth—Fiction. |
    Teenage pregnancy—Fiction. | Parent and teenager—Fiction. | Suburban
    life—New York (State)—Long Island—Fiction. | Long Island (N.Y.)—
    Fiction. | LCGFT: Novels.
Classification: LCC PS3563.C355 T5 2023 | DDC 813/.54—dc23/eng/20220909
LC record available at https://lccn.loc.gov/2022043524

Our books may be purchased in bulk for promotional, educational,
or business use. Please contact your local bookseller or the Macmillan Corporate
and Premium Sales Department at 1-800-221-7945, extension 5442,
or by email at MacmillanSpecialMarkets@macmillan.com.

Picador® is a U.S. registered trademark and is used by Macmillan Publishing
Group, LLC, under license from Pan Books Limited.

For book club information, please visit facebook.com/picadorbookclub or
email marketing@picadorusa.com.

picadorusa.com • instagram.com/picador
twitter.com/picadorusa • facebook.com/picadorusa

1 3 5 7 9 10 8 6 4 2

For David
and in memory of Paul Briand

Part
One

THAT NIGHT WHEN HE CAME to claim her, he stood on the short lawn before her house, his knees bent, his fists driven into his thighs, and bellowed her name with such passion that even the friends who surrounded him, who had come to support him, to drag her from the house, to murder her family if they had to, let the chains they carried go limp in their hands. Even the men from our neighborhood, in Bermuda shorts or chinos, white T-shirts and gray suit pants, with baseball bats and snow shovels held before them like rifles, even they paused in their rush to protect her: the good and the bad—the black-jacketed boys and the fathers in their light summer clothes—startled for that one moment before the fighting began by the terrible, piercing sound of his call.

This is serious, my own father remembered thinking at that moment. *This is insane.*

I remember only that my ten-year-old heart was stopped by the beauty of it all.

Sheryl was her name, but he cried, "Sherry," drawing out the word, keening it, his voice both strong and desperate. There was a history of dark nights in the sound, something lovely, something dangerous.

One of the children had already begun to cry.

It was high summer, the early 1960s. The sky was a bright navy above the pitched roofs and the thick suburban trees. I hesitate to say that only Venus was bright, but there it was. I had noticed it earlier, when the three cars that were now in Sheryl's driveway and up on her lawn had made their first pass through our neighborhood. Add a thin, rising moon if the symbolism troubles you: Venus was there.

Across the street, a sprinkler shot weak sprays of water, white in the growing darkness. Behind the idling motors of the boys' cars you could still hear the collective gurgle of filters in backyard pools. Sheryl's mother had already been pulled from the house, and she crouched on the grass by the front steps saying over and over again, "She's not here. She's gone." The odor of their engines was like a gash across the ordinary summer air.

He called her again, doubled over now, crying, I think. Then he pitched forward, his boot slipping on the grass, so it seemed for a second he'd be frustrated even in this, and once again ran toward the house. Sheryl's mother cowered. The men and the boys met awkwardly on the square lawn.

Until then, I had thought all violence was swift and surefooted, somehow sleek, even elegant. I was surprised to see how poor it really was, how laborious and hulking. I saw one of the men bend under the blow of what seemed a slow-moving chain, and then, just as gracelessly, swing his son's baseball bat into a teenager's ear. I saw the men and the boys leap on one another like obese, short-legged children, sliding and falling, raising chains that seemed to crumble backward onto their shoulders, moving bats and hoes and wide rakes that seemed as unwieldy as trees. There were no clever D'Artagnan mid-air meetings of chain and snow shovel, no eye-to-eye throat grippings, no witty retorts and well-timed dodges, no winners. Only, in the growing darkness, a hundred dumb, unrhythmical movements, only blow after artless blow.

I was standing in the road before our neighbor's house, frozen, as were all the other children scattered across the road and the sidewalk and the curbs as if in some wide-ranging game of statues. I was certain, as were all the others, that my father would die.

Behind us, one of the mothers began to call her husband's name, and then the others, touching their throats or their thighs, one by one began to follow. Their thin voices were plaintive, even angry, as if this clumsy battle were the last disappointment they would bear, or as if, it seems to me now, they had begun to echo, even take up, that lovesick boy's bitter cry.

They had first appeared just after dinner. Three cars—hot rods, we were still calling them then (not one of us imagining the phrase to be more than descriptive, never considering it somewhat obscene)—turning onto the north end of our block, moving slowly, steadily. I had just joined my parents on the front porch. I saw my mother raise her chin to look over the wrought-iron railing and the rhododendron bush as each car stopped at our corner, one waiting patiently for the next, like cars carrying beauty queens in a stalled parade, and then, just as slowly, carefully, they turned to the right.

We could see they were full of teenagers; there was an impression of black leather elbows at each window, black hair, sunglasses. No radios were playing and so only the sound of the straining, impatient motors seemed threatening. Like a big man snoring, I thought, or a dog growling in his sleep. I can't recall at all the cars' colors or their makes. A Chevy of some sort, no doubt, say turquoise or sky blue, then a dark one, say a dark green Ford with tinted windows (and the tinted windows must be true because Sheryl's boyfriend was in that second car, pressed into the back seat between two others, and none of us saw him until the cars, after who knows how many slow circuits of our street, suddenly turned with a sound like an explosion and drove onto her driveway and up over her lawn), the third perhaps a white Buick with one long red stripe that ended in a pitchfork or maybe a devil's tail.

When they approached a second time, about ten minutes later, again turning onto the far end of our street and still maintaining that patient, creeping speed, my mother said, "Uh-oh."

As the last car once again rounded our corner, making a left this time, I saw Sheryl's neighbor, Mr. Rossi, standing at his front door. He wore a T-shirt and suit trousers and held a folded newspaper in one hand. His short, thick arms were both stained with darkening tattoos. He turned away only when the low rumble of their engines, which did not change even after they'd left our block, had faded completely.

I once thought they had been wise to maintain this slow speed even after they'd left our street, to slowly cruise a dozen blocks, to spread suspicion up and down the neighborhood, dissipating it, but now I wonder if they would have avoided suspicion altogether if they'd taken off, back-fired, burned rubber.

This was not an especially rough town, but by then its residents must have simply resigned themselves to hoods and gangs and hot rodders, to teenagers in trouble, the way the first frontierspeople must have resigned themselves to an occasional Indian raid, an occasional outlaw who shoots up the saloon. At that time, in our town at least, it was a given that hoods bombed around, intimidated the band members who tried to get past them into the pizza parlor, drank beer. Word was that some of them poured gasoline over stray cats and set them on fire, screamed "Fung-goo-la" into old ladies' bedroom windows in the middle of the night, smoked reefer—that one had pulled and used a knife on a geography teacher (something I recalled only years later, when our university announced it was cutting the entire geography department), that another had run his car into the dry cleaner's window, but essentially, they were innocents. When they got out of hand the police could be called and, without nightsticks or tear gas, scatter them.

On the night he came for her, it was the uncharacteristic speed, the calm, that made us take notice. It was their order, their odd control (they all sat still inside their cars, looking straight ahead) that made my mother say as they passed a third time, "This is ominous."

My father looked over his newspaper.

Next door, Mrs. Evers had brought her garbage to the curb (her husband would later carry the lid like a shield into the battle) and now stood with her hands on her hips, watching the cars as they passed, one, two, three, through the stop sign and, this time, down the next street.

She turned, saw my parents, and slowly climbed our steps. She was a big woman, freckled, pot-bellied, her belly split like a backside by her caesarean scars. She was famously homely around our neighborhood, not so much because of her looks, which were plain enough, but because of her husband's. Mr. Evers was exquisite, handsome in that chiseled Hollywood way that could make even the oldest mother suddenly shy, and it was the speculation regarding why a man who looked like that would have married a woman who looked like this that had transformed poor Mrs. Evers from not good-looking to our very code word for ugly.

She had four sons, one my age, the others younger, all of

whom later swelled into monstrous adolescence, went on to become bouncers and third-rank football players and, my brother sometimes said, retaining walls. It was Georgie, her oldest, who had cried so terribly beside me as the fighting began.

She had dark hair and a wide, pitted face. It amazes me to think she was only about thirty then.

"What are those kids up to?" she asked us.

My mother shrugged. "They just keep driving past."

"Joyriding," my father said, his tone indicating that it would be silly to make any more of it. Once, in order to illustrate how one bad habit can completely destroy your good name, he had told me how he had happened to see Mrs. Evers push her fingernail up into her nose, examine it, and then put it into her mouth. I myself had already seen her do this any number of times—stretched in her chaise by their aluminum pool, reading the newspaper with one hand—but now the gesture took on the significance of his moral and I could no longer look at the woman without disapproval.

Mrs. Evers stared at the street as if the three cars were passing once more, although—and I had begun listening for them now—they were nowhere near.

"They're going so slow," she said.

"Maybe they're teaching each other to drive," I offered. I used my father's "Why worry?" tone, hoping he'd catch my disdain.

I suppose they ignored me. Mrs. Evers again looked down the street. "I just hope," she said, scraping a piece of her dinner from between her teeth with yet another fingernail, "it doesn't have anything to do with Sheryl."

I caught my mother's look: a pinch between the eyes, her mouth shriveling to the size of a dash. I saw her wrestle for a moment with her desire to protect me from what she considered the sordid details and her desire to gossip.

"He knows she went away?" she whispered, the whisper a kind of compromise, I suppose. "Doesn't he?"

Mrs. Evers shook her head, but said, "I don't know. They had to have their number changed. He was calling."

My mother put her hand over her heart and looked at Sheryl's house across the street and three houses over. It was much like all the rest, brick and shingle, no front porch like ours, but four front steps and, under the front window, an odd hedge, dead in spots and in need of trimming. At that time, everyone in our neighborhood was painting their bricks red or white, or, in a scattered kind of houndstooth, a little of both, but Sheryl's house still had plain dull brick-color bricks—they looked somewhat dusty in comparison— and I took this as an outward sign of her household's one distinction: Sheryl's father had died the spring before; she, her mother and grandmother lived there alone, as everyone put it, meaning without a man in the house.

Their front door was wide open that night behind the aluminum screen door, as were the front doors all up and down that side of the street on this, on every, warm summer evening. We could see just faintly the white stair steps beyond the door. There was a window fan, a blur in the front upstairs window.

My mother put her hand to her heart and looked at the house, and I looked with her. It could not have seemed more forlorn, more unprotected.

"I'm sure they told him she's not there," she said.

"I hope they told him," Mrs. Evers said, sucking her teeth. "He's a troublemaker." She nodded emphatically at the word, for Sheryl was indeed "in trouble" and surely he had made it.

My mother shook her head. "None of those cars is his."

Mrs. Evers was halfway to her own side door when the faint guttural sound of their approaching engines came upon us again.

Now curtains in other windows began to stir. Mr. Carpenter, our neighbor across the street, paused while setting a sprinkler out on his lawn. His wife appeared in the window behind him.

I noticed this time that when the first car stopped at the corner, the second stopped just past Sheryl's house, the third just in front of it. No one in the cars turned to look at her house, at any of our houses, and yet it was easy to imagine that despite what seemed a steady forward pace, it was before and around Sheryl's house that they lingered.

When they had passed, my mother mentioned this. My father, who this time had watched the full progress of the cars down our street, the paper for once forgotten, said, "You could just as well say they're interested in our house. All their cars stop in front of us, too."

I saw that the young childless couple who lived next to the Everses—they had what the other women in the neighborhood called "the unlikely name of Sunshine" (always tagging the accusation with a mouthed "Jewish," as if that both explained the name and made it even more unlikely)—were now out on their driveway and that Mr. Meyer, who lived on the opposite corner, was already on his porch.

I looked again at Sheryl's house. There was only the spinning fan, the pale shadows behind the thin screen door.

The sun by this time was just below the houses across the street, but not yet low enough to give any real hint of darkness. Since it was a usual night except for the cars, other children had begun to come out. I remember the Meyer twins tossed a ball on their front lawn. Billy Rossi crossed the grass between their driveways and was admitted through the Carpenters' side door. Jake, the little retarded boy from the end of the block, rode his bike up our driveway and then, as he did every evening, called for help until my father went down to turn him around. From here and there, the sound of lawn-mowers rose like the staccato drill of locusts.

I don't remember hearing any arguments that evening, none of those strained, echoey exchanges between husbands and wives, parents and children, that made us turn to one particular house as if to a radio, raising our noses as we listened, as if strife were a scent on the air. And as far as I can recall, no neighbors went out looking showered and flushed and, the wives especially, unusually polished, for anniversary dinners or wakes. (Whether these were really the neighborhood's two most common social engagements, I can't be sure. I'm relying now only on my mother's comments. When we saw the wives emerge in silver blue dresses or sequined tops, my mother would say, "It must be their anniversary." If they left the house on a weekday night dressed in simpler Sunday clothes, my mother would say, "They must be going to a wake.") Except for the cars, a usual evening. My parents, as usual, keeping vigil from behind the rhododendron bushes. Enough, too much, has already been said about boredom in the suburbs, especially in the early sixties, and I suppose there was a kind of boredom in those predictable summer evenings. I suppose boredom had something to do with the violent, melodramatic way the men later rushed to Sheryl's mother's aid. But I remember those nights as completely interesting, full of flux: the street itself a stage lined with doors, the play rife with arrivals and departures, offstage battles, adorable children, unexpected so-liloquies delivered right to your chair by Mrs. Evers or Mrs. Rossi or whoever happened to climb our stairs. It's nostalgia that makes me say it, that most futile, most self-deluding of desires: to be a child again, but there was no boredom in those suburbs, not on those summer evenings, or at least not until this one. For after this, after the cars and the sudden spinning onto her lawn, the boys with their chains and the fight and the chilling sound of her boyfriend's cry, after this, no small scenes could satisfy us, no muffled arguments, no dinner-at-eight celebrations, no sweet, damaged child, could make us believe we were living a vibrant life, that we had ever known anything about love.

Venus, as I've said, was already bright.

On their fifth or sixth time past our house, my mother said, "Maybe I should call the police."

"And tell them what?" my father asked her.

She considered this briefly. "That they keep driving around."

"Nothing wrong with that," he said.

My mother looked at me. I could tell she didn't want to call. If she'd wanted to, she simply would have gone inside and done it.

"Somebody's probably called already," my father added.

Now we were simply waiting, waiting for the cars to return, for whatever was going to happen to happen. Mr. Rossi was again at his front door, his shirt off and the newspaper now open and loose in his hand. There was a blue television light behind him.

We saw Elaine Sayles walk to the mailbox on the opposite street (my mother swore she only pretended to put something in it) and then stop to talk to Mr. Carpenter, who was now sitting on his front steps with a beer. We saw them both glance up and down the street as they spoke. Mrs. Sayles was a tidy little blonde, the only woman in our neighborhood to wear tennis whites to the supermarket—to wear tennis whites at all, I suppose. She was said to have come from money, although her husband wore gray work clothes and carried a lunchpail. She left him and their three children for Harvard while I was in college, but on that night she was still a silly short woman in a tiny white skirt, flirtatious, nosy, quite capable of merely pretending to put something in the mailbox.

This time when the cars passed, the boy in the front passenger seat of the first one turned full face to us and grinned an enormous Sergeant Bilko grin. He wore sunglasses, maybe mirrored ones. I don't know if he had a counterpart on the other side of the car, but when the last of the three had once again passed, Mrs. Sayles was already hurrying back to her house. Mr. Carpenter, still sitting on his stoop, was beginning to look somewhat mean-eyed.

"She'll probably call the police," my mother said, a splinter of annoyance in her voice.

But the cars passed again: we calculated that they'd just driven around the block; and again, they must have gone to the boulevard and back; and once more: around two blocks, or maybe as far as the grammar school and back. We waited.

Now night was beginning to show itself, along the hedges, in the bushy center of trees. As we waited for them to return, the interval growing longer and longer, becoming the longest yet, we saw Mr. Rossi turn from his door and go back into his living room. We saw Mr. Carpenter crumple the beer can in his hand, stand and, bringing the can to the garbage, look up and down the street one last time. He too went inside, and Mrs. Sayles turned on a light and drew her curtains. We were beginning to spot lightning bugs. Down the block, the Sunshines (who were sportsminded, it was assumed, because they were childless) practiced a few golf swings with an imaginary club, he standing behind her, her arms inside his, and their cheeks together. The Meyer twins began tossing their small pink ball with a vengeance, aiming at each other's thighs. One or two cars passed. The streetlights snapped on. My parents began to discuss something else entirely.

I suppose we all believed that the boys had given up the game; that with the beginning of darkness they had gone on to the highway or to the broader, less peopled territory of the schoolyard or the parking lot outside the bowling alley; that they had grown bored with teasing us, scaring us, laughing at us, and had finally moved on to their real fun, to adventures that we, even as observers, couldn't share.

None of the boys in those cars was more than nineteen or twenty and yet they obviously, maybe instinctively, knew something about courtship. When we finally heard the engines again, that constrained roll and tumble of slow-moving, mufflerless motors, we merely sighed, not daring to smile. We turned our backs to them, tossing our heads like hurt girls, snubbed tramps. Mr. Rossi did not leave his television; Mrs. Sayles's curtain didn't stir.

They traveled in the same order: the blue one followed by the green, then the white one with its red devil stripe or a black flourish shaped like a striking snake.

The first was just at Sheryl's house when all the engines seemed to explode and the cars, as if the road itself had suddenly leaped and tossed them into the air, were over the curb, one on Sheryl's lawn, one perpendicular to it, up over the sidewalk, the third at an odd, twisted angle in her driveway.

My mother grabbed my arm at the sound, pulled me even, as if she would have me run, although both of us were still in our chairs. My father had jumped up, his arms raised, a caricature of rough-and-ready. The other men were already out of their homes.

The car doors—the ones that faced the house—swung open and the boys slid out. They seemed eerily nonchalant; some even stretched, as if they'd simply stopped for gas in the middle of a long trip. Rick was with them, of course, and he strode unhurried across the lawn and up the three steps. He knocked, not violently, more a polite rattle at the screen door, while his friends stood in loose formation by the cars, looking around and behind themselves as if they planned to stay awhile.

It was their calm and his, especially his as he stood there at the front door, waiting for someone to come, his shoulders hitched back, his fingers slipped into his rear pockets, that must have kept us all at bay. We had seen him standing there in just that way a hundred times before; we had seen Sheryl come to the door, seen Sheryl's mother, on countless Saturday nights, greet him and let him in, and even those of us who knew Sheryl was gone, even those who knew why, must have considered the possibility that this was some crude and spectacular rite of hood courtship and that to interfere, to call the police, to run, at this moment, to her mother's aid, would have been foolish, either terribly childish or terribly middle-aged. Except for the sound of the idling motors, the smell of exhaust, the black strip of torn grass, it seemed harmless enough.

I don't know when we would have noticed the chains.

Rick rattled the door again and then cupped his hand to the side of his face to look inside. I thought I saw, but only faintly, Sheryl's grandmother appear on the stairs. And then her mother was behind the screen.

There was some exchange of words. Sheryl's name must have been heard by the boys scattered around the lawn, by the neighbors standing nearby. Rick suddenly glanced up at the house; his movements for the first time somewhat abrupt, nervous. He said something else through the screen and then quickly grabbed at it, pulling it open. He spoke again, as if the opened door would give him more meaning. We saw him lean inside, his foot on the threshold. His voice grew louder, but his words were still unclear. Then, in one swift movement, he pulled Sheryl's mother through the door. He was holding her forearm. I remember she wore green Bermuda shorts and pale blue bedroom slippers. He swung her around and off the steps. She fell with her arms out, the dry hedge catching her hips and her legs. I don't know if she screamed, but at almost the same moment she fell, the front door slammed—the real door this time, not the screen—and Rick began to yell.

Now the men in the neighborhood were running to their garages, calling to one another with what I remember only as sounds, sounds with lots of *go*'s and *ca*'s. "C'mon," I suppose they said. "Let's go." My father answered in kind, barking one syllable from our porch and then rushing past us. My mother, who still had a death grip on my arm, said, "Go call the police."

Rick had kicked the door and then run down the steps, yelling for Sheryl. He sidestepped across the lawn, looking up to the bedroom windows, to the one spinning fan. Her mother cried, "She's not here," and he looked down at her, made as if to kick her, and then, spinning around, called again. He was bouncing now, almost jiggling. He moved backward across the lawn, looking up at her house, yelling for her. You could hear the men running in the street. You could hear the boys gathering up their chains.

Rick bent as if he might fall, danced a little and then drove his fists into his thighs. His cry rose above the idling engines, the footsteps, the hum of backyard filters and window fans, the hard sounds that passed between the running men. For just one second before the fighting began, it was the only sound to be heard.

WHILE WE, THE CHILDREN, ROAMED through our neighborhood like confident landlords, while we strolled easily over any lawn, hopped into any yard, crossed driveways and straddled fences as if all we surveyed were our own (looking shocked and indignant when someone suggested otherwise, or simply smiling ruefully, dismissing some adult's demand to stay off the grass as we would any bad idea), while our mothers knew the kitchens and dining rooms and side doors of any number of our neighbors and could chat as casually on a street corner as in a breakfast nook, our fathers, until that night, were housebound and yardbound. Once their cars had delivered them home each evening, they might be seen puttering on the lawn or taking the garbage to the curb or sitting on their porches, but until that night, the night of the fight, the sidewalks for them might have been like those two closet-sized bedrooms in each of our homes, might have been meant for children only, meant only as a place to line up for the school bus, to push a doll carriage, to ride a bike until you had grown coordinated enough to ride in the

road. Seen out upon them, usually late at night and usually with
a dog, our fathers seemed huge and foolish, like fullbacks on tricycles. They smoked cigarettes, hunched their shoulders, hugged
the curb. They walked quickly and quickly returned to touch home.

But in those days that followed the fight, all that changed. In
the days that followed the fight, our fathers stepped out of their
houses and over their property lines. They drew together as only our
mothers had done before, meeting each other as if by chance at
the curb, the mailbox, the edges of lawns. Some of them still wore
squares of gauze taped over their foreheads or pink Band-Aids
wrapped tightly around every knuckle of one hand, and when they
met they would lift their shirts or raise a pant leg, bending like
farmers to examine each other's wounds. They would reenact in
slow, stylized motion the blows they'd given, the blows they had
received, adding now the grace that had been missing from the
original performance, the witty dialogue, the triumph. They would
talk together until nightfall and the mosquitoes drove us all inside.

Now the children stepped back from what until then had been
their own territory, stepped back and grew silent as children will
do whenever grown-ups join and claim their games.

On the first of these evenings, the men gathered at the foot of
our own driveway. My mother and father had been sitting out on
the porch. Diane Rossi and I were on the steps below them, talking
listlessly of what we would like to do with the evening, wishing, as
we were always wishing, that there were an amusement park with a
roller coaster and a funhouse somewhere nearby. When my father
went down to the driveway to help Jake turn around, Mr. Carpenter stopped polishing his car and crossed the street to greet him. I
heard him ask for my father's opinion: What did he think would
happen to Rick now that the police had him?

My father shook his head. He was still guiding Jake, holding with one hand the curved silver handlebars of his four-wheeler, and he seemed to say something about getting what he deserved. The two men watched the boy list badly as he headed down the sidewalk. Then Mr. Evers crossed his own driveway to join them. He had his hands in his pockets, his pants loose and low on his slim hips. His face was delicately tanned. "A couple of years in the cooler," he said. He held out his hand and one by one drew in his fingers. "Trespassing," he said. "Assault. Attempted kidnapping. Maybe breaking and entering." His good looks added authority to his words, as if he were reading them from a script. The other two men nodded, their eyes on him.

Diane and I had also grown silent. Behind us, my mother had placed her magazine on her lap and turned her head away from the men as if she were contemplating some article she'd read, not eavesdropping.

"He hasn't got a record," I heard my father say.

"He does now," Mr. Carpenter told them.

Jake Sr. approached. He had Daisy, their beagle, pulling furiously on the end of a leash. He smiled when they questioned him. He was a tall, thin man and he reminded me of a cowboy on a restless horse the way he moved back and forth, trying to counterbalance Daisy's desperate forward motion. "How about five years on a chain gang?" he said. Their laughter was like a shout.

On the night of the fight, while my father and most of the other men were at the hospital or the police station, I had asked my mother what would happen to Sheryl's boyfriend. Her sigh had surprised me. Just an hour or so before, she had been as shrill with outrage as all the other women, spitting out words like *hoodlums* and *punks*. "I don't know what will happen to him," she'd said, sadly, perhaps even somewhat wistfully.

Later, I heard my father in the kitchen, telling her, "Just a slap on the wrist." I may have grinned with relief. I imagined them releasing him. I imagined him searching the country, trying to find her. I imagined him growing closer and closer, zeroing in. I imagined him taking her in his arms.

But early the next morning, when my father in his short summer pajamas limped across the hallway to the bathroom, I saw that his pale legs were covered with red welts and bruises the color of tea stains and I was suddenly ashamed of my disloyalty.

That evening over dinner, he explained to my brother and me that the men in the neighborhood would get a slap on the wrist from the judge because they had taken the law into their own hands, but the hoods would end up in jail.

Jake broke through the men and once more pumped his bicycle up our driveway. This time, Diane and I helped him turn around. Then we followed him down to the sidewalk and the men. Mr. Rossi had joined them, and so after we petted Daisy (who, unaccustomed to being walked, was now lying exhausted on the grass), we each went to our own father's side.

"To tell the truth," mine was saying, "I don't really care what happens to him as long as they stay away from here."

"They'd better," Jake Sr. said. He had a piece of masking tape on his thick tortoise-shell glasses and I wondered if they'd been broken in the fight. "They'd just better."

Mr. Rossi smiled. "Oh, I think they'll stay away. I think they learned their lesson."

The men all agreed, stirring a little. I feared the subject would be closed—it was closed, I suppose, but the men seemed reluctant to break up. It was a humid night and they were all in T-shirts or shirt sleeves. They stood with their arms folded across their chests, their hands pressed flat under their arms, or, as Rick had stood, with their fingers tucked into the back pockets of their pants. Their skin gave off a warm metallic odor that I associated then with their belt buckles, with the dog tags or Saint Christopher medals they wore around their necks.

"Well, I don't know how we didn't see it coming," Mr. Carpenter said suddenly. He glanced at the others. "With that crowd she ran with."

Again the men stirred with a kind of agreement.

"Saw what coming?" Mr. Rossi said.

I felt my father glance at me. "Her getting herself into that situation," he said softly. He looked at Mr. Carpenter. "Right?"

Mr. Carpenter nodded. "Yeah," he said. "That and the fact that a crowd like that isn't going to let one of their girls just go away."

The men moved again. I had the feeling they were nodding with their whole bodies.

Mr. Carpenter ran a hand over his short red hair. "I don't know," he said. "Maybe we should have seen it coming. We should have said something to her mother."

"If she had her father," Jake Sr. said, and Mr. Rossi interrupted him.

"If she had her father," he told them, "none of this would have happened. You think those punks would have come to the house if there'd been a man there?" He laughed, as if at the foolishness of anyone who would believe such a thing. He was a short, dark man with a flat head, bound for the death of his only son and a middle age spent in sideburns and bell bottoms. "She had her father," he said, "he would have stopped it long before it started."

The men moved again to show they agreed. I tried to remember. Sheryl's father. A thin blond man with high color. Balding. He, too, had been somewhat housebound. I remembered him getting out of his car and getting into it. He had had a heart attack one morning as he drove his car to work.

Mr. Evers said, "I don't know." He might have been speaking to himself, but the other men leaned forward to listen. "She always seemed like a nice kid." He turned to Mr. Rossi. "Your daughter starts dating a punk, what are you going to do? Lock her in her room?"

We all looked at Diane, who seemed a little frightened and yet pleased by the question, as if it were proof that Mr. Evers had designs on her. I tried to imagine her pigtails gone, her short bangs grown down into her eyes, her hair teased into a lump at the back of her head. I pictured her with some teenager's leather arm hung heavily over her shoulder.

Mr. Rossi put his arm around her. "Yeah," he said. "Maybe. If I have to."

"She was pretty," Jake Sr. said suddenly, indicating Sheryl's house with a nod. "Wasn't she?"

The men seemed to consider this. They might have been recalling someone already long gone. And then, one by one, they began to agree. "Oh yeah," they said. "She was a pretty girl." "Sure." They looked toward Sheryl's house, where her mother and grandmother were already packing. Packing their clothes and consoling themselves with the news that the girl had been found in time and so would live: a miracle, of sorts.

"Cute," Mr. Evers said.

I suddenly felt Mr. Carpenter's great hand on my head. He gripped my skull, palming it like a basketball. "Cute as these two gals?" he asked. All the men smiled. There was something proprietary about their looks, as there was about Mr. Carpenter's touch. As if having claimed the sidewalks and the streets, they were now ready to claim the children who used them.

"Just as cute," Mr. Evers said.

Jake Sr. smiled. "Sure."

"Well, then." Mr. Carpenter moved my head back and forth. "We'd better get sharp." He slid his hand down the back of my hair and lightly held my neck between his thumb and forefinger. He had a small daughter of his own who even in adulthood would be known as Little Alice, as if she were a gnome. "We're going to be throwing boys off our lawns for years to come."

"Spare me!" my father cried, grinning.

Mr. Rossi laughed. "We'd better start studying jujitsu."

"Or get a shotgun," Jake Sr. shouted.

As if sensing their enthusiasm, Daisy suddenly stood.

Diane and I looked at one another, both frightened and pleased. What were roller coasters and colored lights, funhouse mirrors and barrels, compared to the nights we would soon experience, suspended over the furious battles of our fathers and our boys?

"I'd kill them," Mr. Rossi was saying. "I'm not kidding." He stepped forward to jab a finger into the center of the circle. "And it would be justifiable homicide, too!"

Mr. Carpenter raised his hand from my neck to say, "I'd make them a present of their balls."

"That's what they deserve," my father said.

Jake Sr. added, "Punks."

My mother called to me and Diane from the porch. Reluctantly, we went to her. "Why don't you stay here and let the men talk?" she whispered. We whined a little, but she insisted and we sat again on the steps. My mother's call had reminded the men to lower their voices and they were speaking softly now, but not so softly that we couldn't hear our names being mentioned, and the names of the other daughters on the block; not so softly that we couldn't hear what they would do to them, those hoodlum boys, how they would protect us.

Our fathers. They were still dark-haired then, and handsome.

Their bruised arms were still strong under their rolled shirt sleeves, their chests still broad under their T-shirts. They had fought wars and come home to love their wives and sire their children; they had laid out fifteen thousand dollars to shelter them. They had grown housebound and too cautious, as shy as infants, but now, heady with the taste of their own blood, with the new expansion of their territory, the recalled camaraderie of men joined in battle, they were ready to take up this new challenge, were ready to save us, their daughters, from the part of love that was painful and tragic and violent, from all that we had already, even then, set our hearts on.

They were wrong about Sheryl, of course. She had not been very pretty. And as time passed, they became even more wrong about her. They said she had been beautiful. They said, when trying to praise another girl's looks, "She is as pretty as that Sheryl was," her name giving the praise an edge of sadness and ill fate, so the listener would often reply, "Let's hope she turns out better," so we all could come to recognize the fine, dangerous line that only pretty girls must walk. Even just recently, while watching the Miss America pageant in the white- and coral-colored living room of her Florida condo, my mother had said of her favorite contestant, "You know who she reminds me of? She reminds me of Sheryl." It wasn't true, but I long ago had stopped trying to push back the tide of her praise.

She was skinny, not very tall, with thin taffy-colored hair and light brown eyes. Her front teeth overlapped each other like dealt cards and protruded just enough to change her lip when she held her mouth closed. Her mouth was small and seemed to hang a little too low in her round flat face. She wore pancake makeup and black eyeliner that itself was sometimes lined with white. She dressed as all the girls who went with hoods had dressed. To school, she wore

tight skirts and thin, usually sleeveless sweaters made of some material like Ban-Lon or rayon and meant to show off both her bra straps
and her small breasts. She wore bangle bracelets and, later, Rick's
silver ID bracelet and a delicate gold "slave chain" on her ankle, under her stocking. She favored thin, transparent Woolworth scarves
in bright red or pale blue and black pocketbooks shaped like small
shopping bags. After school and on weekends, she traded her skirt
for beige or black Wranglers that she had tapered along the inseams
so she would have to lie down on her bed in order to zip the fly. She
kept a teasing comb in her back pocket, the two turquoise spikes of
its handle pointing toward her shoulder blade.

I remember my mother and some of the other women saying
how she had trembled as if she would convulse throughout her
father's funeral. How on the morning he died she'd been driven
home from school by the principal himself. Most of the women
were out on the sidewalk by then, drawn first by the sight of the
police car at the curb and then by the news of what had happened.
They saw her paw wildly at the car door before the principal had
even managed to come to a complete stop and heard her call to
her father, who was by then a good couple of hours dead, as she
ran across the lawn and into the house.

She was the first female child on our block to enter adolescence, but until the night of the fight, I don't remember anyone
taking notice of the fact. During the summer before, her fifteenth
summer, when the sight of her might ordinarily have startled and
touched the men, made the mothers wary and filled us young girls
with envy and awe, Sheryl was marked by a different distinction.
I would see her carrying her books and her pale blue looseleaf
binder home from school, see her boarding the bus for the shopping mall, coming to the door when Rick picked her up for a date
and kissing him good night when he dropped her off, and think

not that these were freedoms and pleasures soon to be my own, but only that these were all things she did despite the knowledge that she would never see her father again.

I was at the age when I believed that if either of my parents died, I would simply die too, would simply disappear, as if with their last breath they would draw me back into themselves, just as they had once told me they had kissed each other and breathed me into life. (Which was not the mere bit of whimsy it may seem. I had asked them what all that heavy breathing they did in their bedroom was meant to achieve.) That Sheryl still lived, that she dressed herself in the morning, ate food, sometimes even smiled, all with her father dead, seemed far more remarkable to me than the fact that she was also growing into an adult.

Apparently, it struck our neighbors the same way: more than our first female teenager, she was our first parentless child.

And Rick, given her fatherlessness, the way she had trembled in her tight skirt and dark stockings, the way her thick makeup had seemed so pathetic on her childish face, bruised with weeping, Rick must have seemed merely a pleasant diversion for the poor girl, maybe someone she could talk to. Not the best boy in the school, but better at any rate (let's face it) than someone like Larry Lawlor, who ate whole sticks of butter, played the clarinet and still, at seventeen, appeared costumeless every Halloween to rattle an orange milk carton in your face and to say in his girl's voice, "Trick or Treat for UNICEF."

Mr. Carpenter was wrong: no one could have seen it coming, could have anticipated the girl's logic, the way she had determined to love. Certainly I didn't, and I was someone, perhaps the only one, she'd taken the trouble to explain it to.

———

They had met sometime during that fifteenth summer, the summer before Sheryl went away and the fight took place. At least they'd started dating then, because they must have known or seen one another in school before that. Rick was two years older, but he'd dropped out or been suspended often enough to end up in many of Sheryl's classes. Still, it was that summer when we first saw them together.

Sheryl had a friend named Angie, who lived four or five blocks away. Early that summer, we used to see Sheryl and Angie, freshly made up and, you could be certain, smelling of Ambush cologne, meeting on our corner at about seven-thirty each evening. They would then walk down toward the schoolyard, their hips bumping, their black shoes scraping over the sidewalk. Early that summer, we would see them come back, too, just after dark. We would hear their voices, made twangy and snappy by the gum they chewed. They would call good night to each other as Sheryl went inside and Angie walked back to her own house alone.

There was a sadness in Sheryl's voice as she called to her friend, one that I associated then with her father's death but that I'm certain now had more to do with her reluctance to see the evening end, to see the children disappear and the lights come on in the houses all up and down the street—lights that would burn her eyes when she stepped inside, that would flatten the room's tables and chairs and make the green living room walls seem as discouraging as the triumph of stupid people. Reluctance to hand over a summer evening to small stuffy rooms and a television and the company of two lonely widows when it is only nine o'clock (Sheryl's mother was strict about her daughter's hours) and the boy you would like to love will be free in the wide world until eleven or twelve.

Sometime in July it must have been, in the deeper, stiller days of the season, Sheryl came home in a car just about the time my parents and I were getting ready to go in. It was a sleek, navy-blue Chevy, and with its motor running, it seemed to tremble by the curb in front of her house as if it thrilled to the significance of this event as much as she did. She let herself out, bent to say something to the driver—we had caught him just briefly as the door opened and the light went on inside: a boy, in sunglasses—and then with a wave of her hand she ran across the lawn to her door. The car tooted its horn, leaped to a start, screeched to a stop at our corner and then tooted again as it took off down the street.

That was the last we saw of Angie.

On Saturday night, when the car returned and Rick got out, my mother said, "Oh, Sheryl has a date," and I should remind her the next time she tells me the chosen Miss America isn't nearly as pretty as the one who looked like Sheryl that she had said it with a kind of gratitude, as if the girl deserved it, after all she had been through, as if the boy were merely being kind.

Late in that summer, just before school started, I brought my pajamas and my pillow to Diane Rossi's house. We stayed awake through most of the Late Show, and when we heard the car pull up outside, we turned off the television and crawled over the bed to the window. Kneeling on our pillows, we could see them walk toward Sheryl's house. Rick had his arm across her shoulder. She held the hand he had draped there. At her steps, they kissed again (It was the first time we'd seen them kiss, but even at that age we knew it was again). I remember how painfully her head seemed to bend back as he leaned over her. She climbed the steps, but after she'd opened her front door, she turned and came back down again. She paused above him. He pressed his face into her chest and she wrapped her thin arms around his head. In the yellow pool of light from her hallway they were nearly silhouettes. Only a bit of light caught his shoe, the pale material of his shirt, her white arms.

Delicately, she turned her head, touching her cheek to his hair. She seemed to sigh or, with a dancer's grace, to softly lift her body and settle it down again with one breath. Then, abruptly, she threw her head back, his face still pressed to her breasts, and looked straight up at the sky. Some light from a neighbor's house seemed to penetrate the fine ends of her ratted hair, seemed to touch her throat and her forehead.

She bent her head again, dipped it back into the shadows, kissed his forehead and lips and throat in a kind of blessing, turned and went inside.

He moved quickly once she had closed the door and again tapped his horn as he pulled away, setting someone's dog barking.

Diane and I sank down into our pillows. We could feel the warm night air on our faces. We could smell the summer dust on the windowsill. We could hear her brother, Billy, his summers numbered, snoring in the next room. I think we must have gone right to sleep.

In the days that followed the fight, and they were all hot days, humid and cloudless, the front door of Sheryl's house remained closed and only the shades in the front window, opened in the morning, pulled down in the evening, hours before it was time to turn on a light, reminded us that her mother and grandmother still lived there.

In the middle of one hot afternoon, a black car with a blue police light on its dashboard pulled into the driveway and a man in a thin, somewhat shiny blue suit got out. He wearily climbed the steps, rang the bell and then rapped on the aluminum screen door. We saw him reach into his inside coat pocket as he waited, saw when Sheryl's mother came to the door how he held his wallet up to the screen. She let him in. There was an Ace bandage around her wrist.

Days later, my mother told me that Sheryl's mother and grandmother were gone. She said she supposed they went to Ohio, where Sheryl was. I'd been outside for most of the day every day and so I imagined they'd left very early in the morning, maybe before dawn. I imagined them running between the house and the car like fugitives, rolling quietly down their driveway, turning on their headlights only when they'd reached the boulevard.

I wonder now what heartache it caused them, the mother especially, fleeing her home like that, the home she had made with her husband. I wonder now how bitterly she had looked back across the year and a half that saw her lose her husband, her daughter, her home. With what envy she had looked at the other houses along our block as she drove past them for the last time that morning. How peaceful, how untouched they must have seemed to her, those houses where the brave men slept, their wives tucked under their arms, their children nearby.

Or perhaps as she drove past the shuttered houses, with their damp lawns and purring window fans, she saw instead how precarious their peace was, how momentary. Maybe she saw instead the coming troubles: the scattering of sons, the restlessness of wives, the madness of daughters. Maybe she was aware, in her flight that early morning, that all futures were as uncertain as her own, that even as she drove away, her mother crying quietly beside her, the very blood that pulsed through their veins and set the rhythm that kept their wives asleep was moving pain and age and sorrow to the hearts of the good men.

The house remained empty all the rest of the summer. A police cruiser passed by twice a day and, according to my parents, twice every night. We had all been forbidden to go near the property, and although I had once, on a dare, run up the driveway and rung the side bell, it wasn't hard to keep us away. Up close and face to face, the house seemed sad, but if you pretended to forget it or let it remain in the corner of your eye as you teased Timmy or George Evers or flirted with Billy Rossi or Billy Carpenter, it seemed almost thrilling, almost like a dare. A reminder of the risks and pitfalls of a journey we were taking only the first, tentative steps toward—one that would give us the power for the first time in our lives to bring our entire family to ruin.

Just before Halloween, the Meyer twins tried to start a rumor that Sheryl and her mother and grandmother and even Sheryl's baby were still living in the house, in the top, attic, floor, that the police brought them food and clothing in the middle of the night, but none of us would go for it, even when they claimed they had peeked into the kitchen window at three A.M. and seen four eggs boiling in a pot on the stove.

They had gone to Ohio, we were certain of it. And we named the state as if it were another dimension. Ohio. The sound of it shaped like a drain, a well, like a mouth that had opened to receive them. Ohio. We would spend our whole lives in this neighborhood, in these very houses, even, but she, we were certain, would never come back.

I imagined sending a cryptic message to the jail. I imagined him circling the country until he found her.

We were chalking a spiraling hopscotch into the street before my house and the fingers we moved along the tarred road were growing cold. It was mid-November. The dark tire marks in Sheryl's lawn had lost their sharp edges, like scars that had begun to heal. Our fathers were raking leaves, receding already from the summer's men's club, ducking their heads after muffled greetings. Two cars pulled up to her house. A woman got out of one; a couple about our parents' age got out of the other. The three climbed the steps, the couple looking behind and around them as the boys in the gang had done that night. The woman opened the door and then stepped back to let the couple inside. Behind the screen were the white stripes of the stairs. The shades in the living room went up, and after a bit of a struggle (we could see the woman's forearms behind the glass, and then the man's), the front windows groaned open.

The moving vans were there by the first of the year.

THE BOWLING ALLEY in our town was air-cooled: the decal on the door showed the letters capped with blue-and-white glaciers, dripping like mounds of ice-cream. Inside, the cold air smelled of foot powder and warm socks. There was a row of pinball machines in the entryway, a cigarette machine, two mahogany-colored phone booths with seats like Ping-Pong paddles and doors that turned on both a light and a fan when they were pulled closed. As you entered, there was always the seemingly faraway echo of rolling balls and falling pins. There was the sense, especially in the dimly lit area behind the alleys with its wiry carpeting and small square tables, its trophy hutch and padded bar, of a public place striving to become, for an hour or two, a place to call your own: a homey, ingratiating sense matched only by certain movie theaters and the basement rec rooms of some of our neighbors.

From here Rick made his first troubled call, a day or two, perhaps as much as a week, before that night.

He had not seen her at the supermarket where she worked and

where he usually picked her up on summer evenings. The kid who collected the steel carts from the parking lot said she'd already gone home.

He may have thought of driving to her house, but he was young enough to still be wary, even of her: young enough to fear that any change of routine could portend a sudden and inexplicable change of heart. He drove instead to the bowling alley, where he knew his friends would be. He called from there, the fan whirring above him, the distant sound of the balls and the pins like that of a battle heard from across a wide sea.

Her mother's voice was sad and determined. Sheryl wasn't there. There was no saying when she'd be in.

He rubbed his palms on his thighs before he left the booth, and outside he began to shrug even before his friends had turned to see him. "I don't know where the hell she is."

"Shopping," one of them said.

In a taunting voice, "Maybe she's buying you a present, Ricky."

Only the thickest of them failing to imagine the worst, what was coming for him: the end of the romance.

He stayed with them long after the hour he usually drove off alone with Sheryl. He leaned against his car, one foot hooked back onto the bumper. He grew impatient with their conversation, yet discouraged them when they said, "Let's move." He called her again. The summer-league bowlers had begun to play, and through the glass panels of the booth he could see the backs of their bright, identical shirts, foolish and indifferent—Mr. Carpenter and my father among them. He let the phone ring twenty-three times and then hung up and dialed again. Now it was busy.

He left the booth before he could imagine her: carefully regarding the receiver.

Outside, some girls had arrived and he questioned each of

them—quickly, not even attempting to seem casual, but making sure that tomorrow, when she rejoined him, he would not be ridiculed. They shrugged. None of them knew Sheryl better than he did.

At midnight, with all of them waiting for him in their cars, he called again. Her mother said this was no time for a boy to call. They were all in bed. She would not wake her.

In the bowling alley, the stale cool air seemed hardly to exist, except as a smell and a chill from no particular source. Outside, without a breeze, only the summer heat, the lingering odor of sun-warmed parking lot, of cars and litter, he might have felt this sudden silence had stopped whatever it was that turned and refreshed the earth.

Like most kids who can't get along in high school, Rick had trouble at home. His mother was a strong woman with frail sensibilities who had decided on a fairly regular basis throughout his childhood that she would prefer not to live. She would then either swallow a bottle of aspirin or a box of baking soda or gather up as much cash as she could, combing the house for lunch money and pocket change, and leave town, often with a baby in the crib and the other children still in school. She would choose obscure, unpredictable routes: board a bus for Baltimore or Pittsburgh or take a train to some wealthy suburb of Connecticut or New Jersey. She would check into motels that faced six others on busy interstates or find a place that was an anomaly to its area: a tiny motor inn in a declining middle-class development, an eight-room hotel over a beauty parlor in a small working-class city.

Rick's father was a doctor then, although he'd long stopped practicing by the time Sheryl came around. He was a tall, heavy-boned man, either weary or kind, and he somehow brought his wife back home or back to life every time. Once or twice there had been a piece in the local paper: "Doctor's Wife Sought / Doctor's Wife Found," but apparently the last, discreet line of these articles, "Mrs. Slater was reported missing once (twice, three times) before last year (January, month) and was once (twice, three times) again returned to her home," became too vexing to compose. Or perhaps the editor realized that this was simply the difficult, enduring stuff of daily life, not news, and so the less said the better.

When Sheryl met Rick, his mother was in a flexible mainstreaming program at the state hospital and was home most weekends, "doing okay," her need to disappear or die somehow met by the distance between the sprawling campus of the hospital and the untidy lawn of her four-bedroom house.

Rick's father by then was almost always on crutches. A botched disc operation the same year he had abandoned his failing practice had set off a slow deterioration that subsequent operations only momentarily forestalled, as if the brief recoveries they brought about were mere missteps in the steady progression of his decline.

There was some money from a lawsuit, and at the time Sheryl knew Rick, his father was working for a local medical lab. Two of Rick's sisters had married strangers before they were twenty, and a third took care of things at home and worked part-time in a department store at the mall.

I have never quite gotten straight what happened to Rick's father's medical career. My mother had visited him once, when I was young, as she had visited every doctor in the phone book in those days, wondering what had happened to her talent to conceive, but she only made the connection months after that night. His office had been in a part of our town that had somehow escaped new development if not rezoning and so still retained a battered and incongruous trace of the farm. There were two or three people who still kept chickens in that area, and here and there you could still find narrow wooden-frame houses, some of them abandoned, with old wells and useless water pumps in their tiny yards. Dr. Slater's office was one of these. A green-shingled place with a grape arbor and a sloping porch caught, as touches of paint and threads of old carpeting might be caught in the corners of renovated houses, between a drive-in Dairy Barn store and a stucco ranch given over to card reading and TV repair.

He was a GP, but according to my mother approached his profession with the pride and the disdain of a haughty artist. He wanted nothing to do with money, either taking it in or paying it out. He hired no nurse, no receptionist, no interior decorator to choose couches for his waiting room or paintings for his walls. He used the kitchen and the dining room of the old house for his office and examining room and lined the living room with unmatched stuffed or stiffback chairs. A handwritten index card on the front door told what time he'd be there, and patients simply arrived with their own magazines and ashtrays and waited their turn. He would stay for as long as it took to see everyone, sometimes letting patients into the dining room long after midnight.

When my mother's visit had ended, she had asked him if he would send her the bill. He seemed offended, she said, or embarrassed, and gruffly told her, "Six dollars." He took out his wallet to make change, and when he saw that he didn't have enough singles, made it five. He put the cash in his wallet and the wallet into his pocket, as if, my mother said, he would spend it at the grocery store that very evening. As he probably had.

What his intentions in all this were, no one was sure. A kind of purity, I suppose—medicine alone, medicine as it might have been in older, simpler days of the American frontier, or in some suburban doctor's dream of it. A one-man effort at National Health. My mother had liked him, although the stark and dusty waiting room and especially the old yellow refrigerator she had stared at while he examined her had startled her a bit. When she went back to him a second time, every chair in the living room was taken and people were standing out on the porch. She had me and my brother with her then and had neither the time nor the endurance to wait. She went to another doctor, one with a motherly nurse/receptionist and an appointment calendar and a collection of his own paint-by-number oils on the bright walls, and never returned to Dr. Slater again.

I suppose it's possible that his other patients did the same, as the low fees and the down-home feeling gradually lost their novelty or as the doctor's obvious lack of prosperity began to seem to them a reflection of his skill. Or maybe his scorn of paperwork got him in trouble with the IRS or the AMA or the local hospital. Perhaps his mad wife drove the patients away; or his own wistful and deliberate pursuit of a time that had never been his to begin with had finally appeared even to him as another kind of madness. It hardly matters. His back went out and his operation went haywire. His practice ended.

On the night of the fight, the night Rick came to claim her, he was home with his eldest daughter, who had just returned from her job at the store. She answered the phone, still in her stockings and dress, her name tag still pinned to her collar. He got up slowly, a big man with pale, heavy limbs. He leaned against tables and held on to walls as he made his way to the telephone. His daughter put out her arm for him. Her pity at times like this seemed cloying.

More trouble, he must have thought when he heard his boy's muffled, sullen voice. More bad luck. At some time during that night he must have thought it overwhelming, the bad luck, the series of mistakes that plagued his family. His wife on the edge of some hotel bed in a strange city, her pocketbook on her lap, her eyes passing over him. His youngest daughter already trapped in a bitter, childish marriage; the middle one pregnant and broke, on the road somewhere with her brute; the oldest steeped in a dutiful loneliness. And now his intense and restless son playing out some B-movie drama over the love of a skinny girl.

He must have wondered at some point if they drew the bad luck to them, even unwittingly welcomed it. Or if they were simply, merely, hopelessly badgered. Plagued by invisible, arbitrary demons, by chance alone. Always in the wrong place at the wrong time, the place where a thousand others before them had stood unharmed.

Or is it only that their bad luck seems all of a piece only in the recounting of it?

Would it have seemed to him, even on that night, that his family's history of misfortune was, if not fair, at least reasonable—the good with the bad—when held beside, scattered among, all the days when his wife was well and his children untroubled, when his patients waited for him on the porch of the small house, watching the sunset, smelling the grass, speaking softly to one another as neighbors should. Would it have seemed to him, even on that night, more appropriate to ask, as Sheryl's mother might have asked the morning she fled our street, as lucky as whom? Whose luck is unending? Whose luck has lasted as long as mine has, till now?

When the phone rang that night, he was watching the way the living room light played prettily over his daughter's plain features. She was telling him about a customer and laughing. Her toes in their shiny stockings were round and perfectly shaped. The room, which she had polished and vacuumed that morning, had finally given up the day's heat and grown cool. He was thinking about his wife, who would be home again on Friday, doing better, and how he had loved her when she was his daughter's age. Loved her the way Rick loved his girl now: crazy cross-eyed with it, a little unreal. He had finally found a good position on the couch and for the past hour or two had felt no pain.

When Rick called Sheryl's mother again the next morning, prepared to be relieved, she said her daughter had gone out for the day. He would have recognized the change in her voice from the night before. The night before, she had been hesitant, a little curt, but now she used the sure tone of a person who has long and gleefully rehearsed the way to say, "Gosh, I hate to tell you this . . ."

"She said if you called I should just say she'd gone out for the day. I don't know where she's off to, Rick. You know I've never made her tell me her every move. You know that."

He went to the supermarket, but they told him she hadn't come in to work. He headed for the mall. Neither of their birthdays was coming up, and their one-year anniversary had already passed. What surprise could she be planning for him; what present was worth all this?

He was young enough to fear that he had simply become un-lovable to her overnight, and he began his search casually, self-consciously, just in case it was true. Just in case somewhere someone was watching him, someone who knew.

He walked slowly through the mall, his arms loose at his sides, the sun warm on his shoulders and hair. This was in the earlier days of shopping malls, when they still attempted to resemble cluttered Main Streets, not sealed airplane hangars and Disney World bazaars. There were large concrete planters regularly spaced down the center, filled with hedges and begonias and sad-looking trees. Some were surrounded by small groups of teenagers, who held cups of soda or slices of pizza wrapped in greasy wax paper. The girls wore pale, chalky lipstick, their hair teased, some had pink or turquoise combs slipped into the back pockets of their jeans. He scanned them all quickly—he would know her in a second. He would put his hand to the back of her neck, "Where the hell you been, babe?" If he saw her with someone else, he'd just walk by. Hope his legs would hold him until he got to his car.

He looked carefully into the shoe store, where the customers, lined up neatly in their seats, were easy to see through the plateglass windows and doors. He dismissed the paint stores, the men's shops (unless she was buying him a present?), made one quick pass through Sam Goody's.

He began to walk more quickly, sensing she was there but also feeling still the wise, amused eyes of whoever it was who was watching him, knowing the truth. He was young enough to believe that his foolishness, his humiliation in love, could not go unnoticed and once noticed could never be forgiven.

He set his face into a smirk, even chuckled as he pushed through the door of Newberry's. He passed the counter where she sometimes bought earrings, hit the curtain of the instant photo machine. He passed the bins of white and beige pocketbooks whose odor filled the store, of plastic sandals, of discount makeup and perfume. He checked the wall of birthday and anniversary cards.

In Woolworth's, he paused at a table of scarves. They were piled loosely, bright and tangled and so thin that it seemed only their white price tags kept them from rising like smoke into the cooled air. He touched one—a pale yellow with almost colorless white polka dots—and its rough, familiar feel already seemed a reminder of something lost. He had untied the scarves she sometimes wore around her throat. Once, she had draped one across her bare shoulders like a stole.

Again he checked the jewelry and makeup. At the lunch counter, a child had just gotten sick. She stood pale and dazed as her mother seemed to beat at the front of her sunsuit with a wet paper towel. A black janitor was wheeling a bucket and a mop to the spot. The other customers had scattered to either end of the counter.

When he turned away, he found two teenage girls watching him. "Oh, sickening," one said directly to him, and he recognized the invitation. He could talk to her, take her telephone number. He could bury his face in her stiff hair.

"You're ugly," he said and saw her face change, just slightly, as if some small thing behind her makeup had slipped. He left the store.

Now he was jogging. The big stores seemed to mock him with their narrow aisles and invisible doorways, their elevators and dressing rooms. He realized that he could just be missing her at every turn. She could be just on the other side of the mall sitting with her back to the trees, smoking a cigarette. She could stand and wander away just as he left the escalator in Klein's. She could be fingering the very scarf he had touched just as he emerged into the sunlight once again.

He imagined how he would later see it around her throat or her waist, laugh and say, "When'd you buy this?"

She could be on the bus already, headed home.

He called again and caught her mother by surprise. Her voice was cheerfully formal when she said hello. He asked if Sheryl was home yet. There was a terrible pause. "No, Rick," she said. "No, she's not."

At some time during that day he must have driven past her house. No sign of her, of course, but a startling memory of himself as he had been just days before: confidently climbing those steps, Sheryl there even before he had rung the bell. Himself stepping inside without thought or hesitation, without gratitude or, he realized, even pride. He would wait for her to finish drying the dishes or to run upstairs for her purse. He would stretch out in an armchair like the owner of the house, joke with her Polish grandmother like a favorite son. He would be as confident as a married man of how the evening would end.

Just days ago, he climbed those steps and she had been there behind the screen. Although last time she had been ready when he arrived and had not invited him in.

He ate supper with his father and his sister that night, simply to define for himself the beginning of evening, the end of the lousy day.

His sister said, "To what do we owe the great pleasure of your company—run out of pizza money?"

He told her to stuff it, then added that she was becoming a bitchy old maid.

She called him a punk.

He said he didn't see any boyfriends knocking down her door. "When was the last time you had a date?"

She said, "Oh, shut up." But he leaned closer to her as she worked at the sink. He knew, unconsciously, that she would do anything for him. Long ago she had taken up their mother's slack in compassion and care, taken up with a kind of fatalism what she saw as their consequences: she would never be loved sufficiently in return.

"Don't you even wonder what it's like to get laid?" he whispered.

"Go to hell," she said.

"To have some guy slip it to you?"

She was silent, but her cheeks were burning.

"Make you feel so good you want to go crazy."

"Drop dead," she said.

He sighed. "Guess if you've never had it, you'll never miss it."

He turned from her. His father was leaning in the doorway. He had one crutch under his arm, and his free hand grasped the doorframe. "Knock it off, Rick," he said. His father's skin seemed tight on his skull. He seemed to be growing older and thinner by the hour.

"Christ," Rick whispered as he brushed past him. "Nice to be home."

He called again at about eight. Her grandmother answered the phone, and he said quickly, "Can I speak to Sheryl, please?" There was another pause. He could hear muffled voices, the sound of someone putting a hand over the receiver. Then her mother's voice. "Yes?" As if she didn't know who was on the other end.

"Can I speak to Sheryl?" he said again.

She hesitated once more and then simply said, "No, Rick. No you can't. And I think it would be best if you didn't call here anymore."

She hung up before he had shouted his reply. He dialed again, but the phone was once more off the hook. He pounded the metal wall of the booth, pulled open the doors.

"She won't let me talk to her," he told his friends at the pinball machines, his voice cracking with anger. "I'll kill her." He headed for the doors as if that's what he would do. Some of the bowlers had turned around when they heard his shout. His friends put their hands on his chest. He tried to push them away. "I'll kill that old bitch," he said, and they all feared he was about to cry. They got him out the door. He pulled away from them and kicked at his own car. "What the fuck's going on?" he said. "What the fuck is happening?"

Cautiously, they asked if he and Sheryl had had a fight, was there anything wrong between them. He shook his head. "No," he said. "No, man, it's her old lady. It's that old bitch."

He said it to protect himself, no doubt, to keep from having to admit to them that he feared everything had changed, that he feared she had changed her mind overnight, become, as his mother used to do, another person entirely—one whose strangeness was all the more terrible because of what part of him it hid: she had said she loved him and then become someone else.

His friends, who would have been more comfortable with his anger than with his tears, who would have preferred to say what should be done to the old bag than to offer their condolences over the loss of something as difficult as love, were no doubt willing to agree. Clearly, they said, she was keeping Sheryl from him, the jealous, horny old bitch. She had found out what Sheryl and Rick did. Her own husband had croaked (probably when he put his head between her legs, one of them said—they had left the bowling alley and were now leaning across their cars in another parking lot, drinking beer), so she's jealous that her daughter's getting what she'll never get again, not unless she pays somebody. Sure, they said, that's what's going on. It's the old lady, trying to make Rick think Sheryl's stepping out on him. Probably keeping her locked in her room till Rick finds somebody else. Sure, that's what's going on.

They shook their heads. They believed it. They had heard enough stories about bitter stepmothers and ugly old queens who locked beautiful girls in dungeons and towers. They were willing enough to see themselves as handsome, persecuted princes whose very rights as men these women would deny.

The familiar, aimless evening took on form, took on drama as they talked. The dark summer trees were thick with it. The dim lights around the parking lot made the black asphalt a stage. They had seen movies with lighting like this. They worked themselves into their best emotions. Isn't this what they'd always suspected: They were persecuted, wrongly accused, unfairly denied. They told the others who joined them what had happened, their voices rising with outrage.

"Gimme a dime," one said, and, to Rick, "What's her number?" The others watched him cross the street to a lighted telephone booth: spotlight. He dialed and hung up and dialed again. He came back. "She must still have the phone off the hook."

Three others jumped in a car and took off. Minutes later, they returned with the news that there were lights on in Sheryl's house, in the living room and in one window upstairs. Another went to the phone: still busy.

"Call Angie," someone said.

Now the grouping of cars had become a command post. When the girls arrived, they stood to one side, looking sympathetically at Rick, who had once again become possible to them, more possible than ever, hurt as he was, or would soon be (because none of them believed Sheryl's mother was keeping her from him—they had mothers, too; they knew it couldn't be done).

Word came back that Angie and a friend had gone to the nine o'clock movie. Two boys were dispatched to wait for them outside.

Someone dialed Sheryl's number again. The plan in the beginning was to ask for her politely; if questioned, to say, "I'm in her math class at school and I thought I'd say hello since I haven't seen her all summer." But as the hour grew late, they decided they would simply curse into the phone, "Listen, you old bitch."

Rick was drunk by now and growing morose. By now he no longer understood what had happened to him—not merely in the past twenty-four hours, but in the past twelve months. She had said she loved him. She had promised him things he could hardly understand except as some kind of fulfillment of all that he knew he wanted, and then become someone else.

His two friends returned from the movies. They'd found Angie and her girlfriend, but she said she hadn't seen Sheryl in a couple of days. She and Sheryl weren't that friendly anymore anyway.

Rick leaned against one of the girls who had pulled herself up onto the hood of his car and his arm pushed into her thigh. "I just hope she's not pregnant," he told her softly. "I just hope that's not it."

Later, he told them that he, and they, should just go right over there and pull her out of the house. Murder the old bitch if they had to. They agreed, but not tonight, they said. They needed a plan.

He drove himself home a little after three. He lightly side-swiped a car parked in the street, scraping paint. He called her again from the phone in the kitchen. This time it rang and her mother answered with a gasp, as if she had just struggled up out of the water.

"C'mon," he said—he would not remember this in the morning—"let me talk to her. Come on." But she hung up on him without a word.

It's hard not to think of Sheryl's mother as cruel in all this: hard not to think of her as the boys did, as the jealous queen, the wicked witch. She was the one, after all, who had swept her daughter out of the state the very day her pregnancy was confirmed, who chose to torment her boyfriend with these coy games. It was she who made sure her daughter had no chance to explain, to tell him good-bye. No doubt Sheryl tried to get past her, tried to call him from the supermarket on the last day she worked, from her own house as she quickly gathered her things together, from the airport, even, when she'd told her mother she wanted to go to the bathroom before boarding the plane and instead headed for the phones. But Rick's house was often empty, or maybe his father couldn't bring himself to move at that moment, or didn't want to try; maybe his sister ignored the ringing phone, certain it wasn't for her.

This isn't news: the world is as indifferent to lovers as it is to the poor and the unlucky. Sheryl's mother would have known this: it's as indifferent to lovers as it is to the dead, and to those who mourn them.

Before her husband's sudden death, she had always been known as a sweet, soft-spoken woman. She didn't pick her nose or pepper her conversations with "Jesus Christ"; she said "sugar" and "fudge" when she drew the wrong cards at canasta, and even the dirty jokes she told were curt and inoffensive. She had curly brown hair and a round, dry face, what I used to think of as gumdrop eyes, as small as buttons.

But at her husband's wake, my mother later told me, she screamed shrilly at a young attendant who placed a small arrangement of flowers on the floor by the casket rather than on a table top, where they clearly belonged. She sent Sheryl out of the room at one point to demand that the funeral director tell the group of Irish people in the next chapel to lower their voices and control their laughter.

"This is a funeral parlor," she said to those who tried to calm her. "Not some shanty gin mill."

In the days that followed, she told the neighbors who asked, "No, there's nothing you can do for me. What in the world can you do for me?"

Our mothers were hurt and puzzled by this. The sudden death of one of the block's husbands had startled them, but Sheryl's mother's anger was even worse. They held their throats as they spoke of it, slid their hand over the kitchen table as if there was something they wanted to straighten and smooth. Their own plans for widowhood, which I sometimes heard them discuss in the same frightened, delighted way we children planned our encounters with vampires and communists, usually involved a gallant, tragic air, a nice secretarial job and the return to the house they'd been raised in. (Although Mrs. Evers, whose parents had both died of the same heart trouble that would eventually, when I was about twenty, free her forever from the risk of becoming a widow, had only cousins to go to.) Never this fury. They shook their heads. I remember them repeating the word *distraught*. I remember thinking that it meant not merely sorrowful but somehow emotionally skewed: you were angry when you meant to be sad, mean when you meant to be grateful; you cried when you were happy.

My father went to her house one evening not long after her husband died to help her with her income tax returns. He came back furious. At one point she had grabbed the pencil out of his hand and flung it across the room. She'd accused him of intentionally trying to confuse her.

"What can you do for a woman like that?" he'd asked.

My mother had shrugged. She seemed a little fearful, as if she were just realizing what being a widow might involve.

"Did she cry?" she asked, and my father said, somewhat indignantly, "She did not." We all shook our heads. There was no forgiving her then.

I think of us as naïve in those days. All of us. Years later, just a few months after Billy Rossi was killed, Mrs. Rossi turned a hose on a couple of little boys who had wandered onto her lawn. No one seemed surprised then, although Mrs. Rossi had always been known as easygoing, even kind. Then we merely shrugged and nodded as if we understood. We said seeing little children, boys especially, was rough for her.

But we resented Sheryl's mother's anger. We said (or our parents said and we children concurred), "She's never going to find another husband with an attitude like that."

We gradually replaced the word *distraught* with *ungrateful* and then *bitter*. Our mothers, who had begun by then to look for reasons to avoid her, said it was high time she pulled herself together and started being pleasant again. How long could they go on feeling sorry for her? How long could one person mourn?

By that summer, she had still not found the courage to look for a job. She had still not learned to change a tire or mow the lawn. She had handed all her finances over to an accountant. Her deliverance, no doubt, took the form for her as much as for us of another husband, but that must have seemed to her as impossible as her loneliness. By that summer she must have realized that she could not mourn forever, or rage forever, that she would have to do something to get on with her life and that still she had no idea what to do.

When Sheryl came into the room that summer morning, her mother was already awake, her hand held over her eyes. In the year and some months since her husband's death, she would have found no change in her sense of loss, or in her disbelief that the loss was hers, but it might have become with each morning more and more difficult to raise the tears that she had thought would wake her for the rest of her life. She might have been remembering some moment from their early marriage, or from their last days together, perhaps some argument they'd once had, turning the memory over and over, searching for whatever it was that would fill her with the appropriate sadness, the only feeling she had become willing to wake for, the only feeling she still feared to lose.

Sheryl appeared in the doorway and said, "Mom," in much the same way she might have said it years ago, hoping to be kept home from school. She wore lacy baby dolls, lavender and white, no makeup, but her eyes still smudged with mascara. Her legs and arms were bony, lightly tanned. Her hair, flattened from sleep, was pressed back behind her ears.

Sheryl walked into the room and knelt on the floor beside her mother, who only turned her head, her hand just lifted off her brow. Reflexively, without tenderness, she reached out to brush the bangs out of her daughter's eyes.

She might once have thought, or been told, that if she lost her husband, her children and grandchildren would save her, but she had learned by then that this simply wasn't true. Sheryl had her father's mouth and full face and something of his coloring, but she was beside the point somehow. Their child, that was all. Another life, not theirs. She was only vaguely aware of the betrayal in this. What, then, were children for?

The light in the pale blue bedroom was the early light of a thousand such summer mornings. The windows were open, and through them came the sounds of the first children, out surveying the grounds, revving up bicycles, me knocking on Diane Rossi's side door.

"Mom," Sheryl said softly, kneeling beside her mother, her hand touching the mattress in some approximation of herself at three, demanding to be pulled into her parents' bed. "I think maybe I'm pregnant."

Her mother rose immediately and went to the phone on what had been her husband's side of the bed. In the months since his death, she had often thought that if it hadn't been so swift and un-expected, so immediately complete, she would have done well. If he had woken her in the middle of the night, clutching his heart, she would have phoned the police, their doctor, the hospital, she would have supervised the attendants who carried him down the stairs and sat calmly beside him in the ambulance. If he'd had cancer or some such slow disease, she would have learned to use hypodermic needles or catheters or whatever he needed. She would have set up a hospital bed in the living room, slept beside him on the couch every night, drawn the curtains and adjusted the pillows so he could see the street, the progress of his lawn (which she would have tended for him), the cardinals and jays perched on the hedge.

She would have proven to him, and to herself, that she was capable. She would have done well.

She asked Sheryl, "When did you have your last period?" and then quickly spoke the answer into the telephone. It was nearly three months ago. She said, "Right away," and checked the bedside clock. When she hung up, she told Sheryl they would see the doctor that morning. Sheryl was now sitting on the bed, her hands in her lap. Her mother went to her then, put her arm around her shoulder, maybe kissed the top of her hair, which smelled of cigarette smoke and hairspray. "Okay," she said. "It will be okay." Thinking already of her sister in Ohio and if it wouldn't be better for Sheryl to fly out there as soon as they knew for sure, maybe tonight.

She took control of her daughter's tragedy in a way she had been unable to do with her own and turned the anger she had learned, the nastiness, to what would have seemed to her to be good use. For in these matters, it was well accepted at the time, the girl must disappear and the hoodlum boy never know.

THAT NIGHT, AS SOON AS I'd managed to break out of my mother's grip, I left our porch and went into the street. All the children were doing it, not even running but almost staggering, somewhat reluctantly, in our fathers' wakes, going only as far as what seemed to be the prescribed borders of the fight: about six feet or so from the cars and her lawn, which left us scattered across both sidewalks on either side and down the middle of the street. When the first police car approached, we merely turned our heads, stricken, I suppose, with that strange paralysis that seems to grip all crying and moaning children. Georgie Evers and I were the first two in his path, and it never occurred to us to step out of his way.

But by then the officer had seen the cars on the lawn and the brawl that took place beyond them.

He stopped, then turned on his siren and his lights, got out quickly and stood dumbfounded for a moment with one foot still in the car and his hand on the open door. He shouted, "You kids," waving his arm (still none of us moved), and then dove into his car again. He turned off the siren, made a call on his radio (the Meyer twins, who stood nearly at his elbow, claimed he said, Mayday! Mayday!), then leaped from the car again, the nightstick in his hand.

But the boys had begun a retreat as soon as they heard the siren. We saw them shaking our fathers from their legs and their arms, dropping their chains and even their jackets to the lawn if that was the only way to get rid of them. Some of the boys were bloodied, the blood black shadows that covered their mouths or their ears. They were shouting each other's names. I saw one of them was lifted and pushed into a car by the others. Car doors slammed. Even as the poor young officer jogged toward the fray, the first car, the one in Sheryl's driveway, the white one with the painted flourish, backed up with a screech and, turning its front wheels over the curb, headed out—passing within inches of some of the children who still stood crying or who, seeing the car come toward them, had leaped into bushes or onto the grass.

Again the cop turned to us and with another wide wave of his hand cried, "Get out of the street." But at the same time, the car that had led the procession did a sudden U-turn across Sheryl's lawn, its horn a staccato yell, and pulled out from her driveway. The next instant, I saw Rick. The light was on inside the remaining car, the one he had emerged from. I saw him through the back passenger window. I almost thought he was turning toward me, but he was simply curling forward in pain. He had lost his sunglasses. His hands, streaked with blood, were cupped over his face. I later learned his nose had been broken, but at the time I was certain he was crying. Then the door closed and the light went out.

While our fathers were still pulling at its doors, pounding at its windows, the car suddenly spit out in reverse and then raced backward down the street, wavering in the streetlight like a fish. Just past the north corner it stopped, darted forward and disappeared.

It seemed the whole world was wailing. In the now nearly total darkness, the sound made you think you should see an orange glow in the sky just beyond the rooftops, see the red flames of some city being consumed by the final conflagration. There was the disappearing siren of the young cop's car, the approaching sirens of his reinforcements, little Jake screaming in his mother's arms. There were the other children, who had been blasted into the hedges and the grass by the escaping cars (and who were lying tragically now, unharmed but unwilling to stand until their own part in the adventure, their own brush with death, had been fully recognized), the children like Georgie Evers, who had never stopped wailing, the mothers who were now running to their battered husbands' sides, even Sheryl's grandmother, who had finally opened the door again and now stood crying in Polish from behind the screen.

It seemed our whole neighborhood had raised its voice in one varied, inharmonious wail.

Amidst all this, I saw my father and Mr. Rossi, who had a glistening gash on his head and on his arm, help Sheryl's mother up the steps and into the house. My mother followed. Just before I caught up with them, I saw Billy Rossi and Billy Carpenter burst out of their driveways on their bicycles, headed in the direction the hoods had gone and whooping like Indians.

Inside, Sheryl's living room seemed soft and comfortable (there were the green drapes and the green carpeting, the small velvet paintings hung high on the walls) and yet at the same time, perhaps because of the plastic slipcovers, sheathed in a thin layer of ice. Her grandmother stood trembling and crying by the single floor lamp, the only light on in the room. She was a small, plump woman. She wore a light cotton shift, her neck and freckled shoulders bare. Her sunken eyes were dark in the dim yellow light. Sheryl's mother sat on the couch. The men were trying to get her to lie down, but she kept saying, "I'm all right, I tell you. I tell you I'm all right," her voice quivering. She was shoeless, and her legs looked clawed. There was dirt on her palms and on her knees. My mother came through the dining room from the kitchen, a glass of water and a wet dish towel in her hands.

"Here, Ann," she said.

Sheryl's mother refused the water but took the cloth and wrapped it around her wrist, sighing and telling them she was all right.

"Mama," she said suddenly and quite crossly to the old woman who stood by the lamp, crying and murmuring, clasping and un-clasping her plump hands. "I'm all right."

I saw my parents exchange a look. What can you do for a woman like that?

Then the police cars pulled up outside, their sirens dying. Their blue lights moved eerily behind the drapes. We heard the doors slam, heard the cops' and our neighbors' voices, heard the spit and sputter of the police radios, those small muttering sounds that seem to accompany all disasters.

A policeman rattled the screen door and then let himself in. Two of them, both large and hippy with their gunbelts and night-sticks. One of them was carrying a small black pad. The other, who was somewhat older, tipped his hat to the ladies and asked their forgiveness for barging in. Sheryl's mother immediately gave them Rick's name and what she knew of his address. The other cop took it down while the older one simply smiled. "We've got one of the cars already," he said. He seemed to be enjoying him-self. "It's not going to be any trouble picking them all up."

Taking a seat on the edge of one of the thick plastic-covered chairs, he leaned forward and in a soft, fatherly voice advised her about pressing charges. She nodded, listening. Yes, of course, of course. The quiver had left her voice.

At one point, my father crossed the room as they spoke and gently took my mother's arm. She was still holding the glass of water she had gotten for Sheryl's mother, and wordlessly, he urged her to drink it. She did, looking all the while like a runner-up in a game with only one perfect prize. (Later that night, after a botched, embarrassed and only sporadically explicit attempt to explain what Sheryl had done, she told me, "Let's just say the stork missed our house and landed on hers.")

When the officer stood again, the plastic slipcovers or his leather holster groaning, he told Sheryl's mother he'd be glad to drive her to the hospital if she wanted to get her legs and her wrist taken care of, have a doctor make sure everything else was okay. He turned to Mr. Rossi, who now held a handkerchief to the wound on his head. He said it wouldn't be a bad idea for him to come along, too.

The cop turned to my father. "You okay?" he asked. My father's shirt was ripped and there was grass and dirt on his pants and in his thick hair, but he said he was fine.

"How about you, tootsie?" the cop said to me.

Involuntarily, I smiled. I had always liked policemen, but now my loyalties were torn.

Suddenly, Sheryl's mother said, "I know you." We all turned to see that she was looking carefully at the officer with the notepad.

"You've been here before," she said. "The day my husband died. He died in his car."

The cop pushed back his hat and said, "That's right," as if he were making a confession. He looked sheepishly at the other men, Mr. Rossi, my father, as if he feared they'd think him a harbinger. "Maybe I can come back sometime when the news is good," he said.

Sheryl's mother continued to study him. Then she said, "No," shaking her head, still not crying. "No," she said.

Outside, the men who were to go to the hospital were easing themselves into the police cars. The others were sitting on the curb or standing on the lawn, waiting to go to the police station. The lawn itself had been badly ripped by the tires and was littered with chains and sunglasses and a leather jacket, but as they waited, our fathers leaned on their rakes or their hoes, Mr. Carpenter crouched beside his upright baseball bat, and so they gave the scene a somewhat wistful portrait-of-America air. They might have been farmers standing over their plowed fields, sandlot baseball stars. Mrs. Sayles, almost luminous in her tennis whites, picked her way among them, offering praise and consolation and cool facecloths.

In the distance, the bells of an ice-cream truck tinkled gaily. Mr. Rossi, still holding a handkerchief to his wound, took a deep breath and told my father to take a look at that sky. "Planets," my father said. He turned to my mother. "You always know which ones are planets." But she refused to look up for him. Instead, she began what was to become the women's second chorus of the night. She put her hand over her heart and whispered, "Stupid kids. Those stupid, stupid kids."

My mother's determination to have another, or as she so often put it, just one more, child had always confused and puzzled me. My brother was born first and then I had been born and it seemed to me her luck in having one of each, both talented and healthy and, in my opinion at least, perfectly formed, should have filled her with gratitude and pride, not longing. And yet, through our thin walls had come the nightly thumping, the hard quick breaths. Listening to them each night, I would imagine both my parents as I had once seen them an hour before the start of one of their New Year's Eve parties: my mother in her slip and her jewelry, my father in his undershirt and good suit pants, puffing frantically into one balloon after another, apparently trying to fill the room. They had seemed to give themselves entirely to each, blowing into it with one long breath (always futilely for the first few seconds, then a miraculous blossoming), quickly examining it, then blowing again. The fruits of their labor, yellow and green and blue and red, bobbing at their feet, bright and useless.

Twice that I remember, my mother had announced that a new brother or sister would indeed arrive, and twice the delicate thing she and my father had managed to form broke without warning. I came home from school to find she was in the hospital for the evening. I was awakened one night by the sound of her voice: every light in the house seemed to be burning, and I found her sitting on the edge of her bed, already in her coat and shoes, waiting for my father to retrieve the fetus from the bathroom.

(Even now in her pleasant and irresponsible retirement, she can say without hesitation how old those children would be today and just where in school or marriage and their careers they might be, had they lived. Even now I'm surprised by the precision and the detail with which she has imagined their lives, and I'm forced to make such calculations of my own.)

That summer, my mother was past forty and in her quest to conceive had begun to resort to what I can think of now only as a kind of voodoo.

Each night she would run hot water into the bathtub before she went to bed and then, when their lovemaking was over, trot from the bedroom to the bath to soak for an hour or two in a solution of Epsom salts or baking soda or whatever powder or potion the other women had advised. Often, my father would go in to keep her company. He would turn down the toilet seat and sit there in his bathrobe, his voice made hollow by the water and the tiles. Sometimes he would read to her from one of her magazines, stories of married women triumphing over various domestic difficulties, reviving their husband's love, rewinning their children's affections, escorting their friends through innumerable tribulations.

In the morning, I would find these magazines on the edge of the tub or the back of the toilet, folded over to the last page and buckled here and there by the dampness, as if the end of each story had been wept over. I would reread them myself to fill in what part I hadn't heard the night before, either because my father's voice had grown too soft or my mother had swished the water too loudly or I had simply fallen asleep before I'd caught the resolution.

In these stories, the women who longed for children got them, usually just as the longing itself had been nearly obscured by something else: a death, a birthday party, an adoption, as if the longing itself had been the culprit. I suppose the message was that too blatant a desire to manipulate your own life was unseemly. I suppose my mother never caught on.

One early morning not many days before the night he came for her, I woke to a kind of drumming sound: hard/soft hard/soft— long interval—hard/soft. In the hallway I passed by my parents' room and through the partly opened door saw my mother attempting a headstand at the foot of their bed. Her head was pressed firmly against the mattress and her hands gripped the spread as if she would tear it, her pale legs kicked up again and again, flailing like arms beneath her white nightgown, one foot hitting the floor each time she was drawn inevitably back to the earth.

I probably would have laughed, rushed in to join them (probably would have offered some good advice), were it not for the serious and determined way in which she tried again and again to raise herself. Were it not for the solemn and somewhat bemused look on my father's face as he watched her from his pillow.

I later learned that it was Leela, Jake's mother, who had advised these acrobatics (meant, of course, to get the sperm moving more swiftly toward its mark). That same summer she and my mother were involved in one of those brief yet intense bouts of friendship the women in our neighborhood so often experienced. They had gotten to talking in the supermarket one morning and for a good number of weeks after were suddenly inseparable. I would smell the smoke from their cigarettes and hear Jake's thick voice as I dressed in the morning. I would see Leela, with Jake on her lap, ride past in my mother's car as I played outside in the afternoon or find her still in the kitchen, Jake's dark head just under the red ash of her cigarette, his cheeks covered with ice cream or cookie crumbs, when I came in from the Everses' pool. In those days, they spent an hour or two on the phone each evening too, talking in low voices that made my father look over his paper to ask me, "They've been together all afternoon, what have they got to talk about?" as if, being female, I would understand.

They talked about conception. Headstands and Epsom salts and vinegar douches that would not only guarantee a baby but a baby boy. They told their life stories. Leela, it seemed, had been married once before. (My mother sharing the news with me on various weekday evenings as she made dinner in much the same way some other lonely woman might have shared it with a bird or a dog, not expecting either response or comprehension, her eyes bright only with the pleasure of repeating what she had heard.) That first marriage had ended precisely because she had not been able to conceive. It was neither of their faults, they were told. It was simply that the atmosphere of her particular womb was inhospitable to his particular seed: an unlucky and insurmountable problem of chemistry. Leela herself had been willing to accept the verdict, had contacted a few adoption agencies and begun sending long chatty letters and eight dollars a month to an orphan in Indonesia, but apparently her husband had been determined to prove the doctors right and, out of nowhere, said my mother, after nine years of marriage, asked for a divorce so he could marry another woman.

My mother slammed pots and let the water in the sink run violently. Forget all that had come before, she said—wielding a serrated knife like a machete—forget the years of their courtship, their big hotel wedding, their first apartment, the hundreds of beds she'd made for him and shirts she'd washed and meals she'd cooked. Forget the headstands and baking-soda baths, the painful and intricate advice, not to mention the humiliating questions, of the pharmacist in her old neighborhood, who had used his white lab coat and mortar and pestle to give credence to the foolish formulas the women themselves brought him: hot-water douches and citrus diets and intercourse performed with your head and throat hanging from the side of the bed. Forget what she had once confided to her husband, believing they were forever bound: if I fail at this, I am neither male nor female; I cannot know my worth. Forget especially that he brought that confidence with him to his new marriage and his young wife.

She'd been barren three years into her own second marriage, already moved into her house down the block, when she finally conceived Jake. She knew, of course, the first time she held him with something like a clear head that he wasn't right, and she momentarily recalled, as the doctor explained, what another had said about her inhospitable womb. But she remembered, too, my mother said, what it had been like to have no child at all.

––––––

On the night of the fight, the night Rick came to claim her, Leela had followed her husband farther than most of the other women had done. She was just in front of the Sunshines' driveway when she stopped to put her hands to her mouth. She wore a white scarf around her bleached blond hair, wore it tied into a bow at her crown because even then, when she had grown chunky and was no longer young, she wanted to look like the GI's dream of Betty Grable. She wore white shorts, a turquoise top that was ringed with perspiration. She called to her husband as the other women were doing, not moving any closer, not making any other gesture to retrieve him, but seeing, no doubt, as the other women saw, the sharp black edge of the hoe he'd lifted as he ran, the threat that had suddenly transformed the night.

And then, just as the first police car arrived and the boys began to retreat, she turned (God only knows, she said in our kitchen the next morning, what made her turn) to see Jake in his pajamas, standing in the middle of the street, the sharkish nose of a car headed toward him. Somehow, she found his arm and pulled it hard, so hard the child screamed and something cracked (although, she said, it may have been a bone in her own jaw). On the sidewalk, she slapped him so fiercely his teeth were bloodied, so savagely that the faint bruise mark of her hand was still there the next morning when I came downstairs and found them both in our kitchen.

Jake was on her lap, a piece of bread crust in his hand. He was grinning and chirping, but she jiggled him on her knee as if he were still wailing. She held a cigarette in one hand and his shoulder with the other. Her nose was running and her eyes were filled with tears. When she saw me, she wiped at her cheek with the heel of her palm.

My mother reached across the table to touch Jake's fist. "But he's fine now," she said, thinking, I'm sure, just as I was thinking, that the child had never been fine.

Their friendship was already beginning to wane. In another week or two, Mrs. Carpenter would have briefly moved into my mother's affections and Leela and Jake once more returned to their own end of the street. I saw her a final time just before my parents' house was sold; and she told me that she, of course, could not leave the neighborhood as nearly everyone else was doing. Jake had a job at the mall and knew how to take the bus there and back. If she or her husband met him at the boulevard each evening, it was safe enough for him to walk home. "If we moved," she'd said, "he'd be losing his whole world."

I saw her raise her eyes to the cloud of smoke that hovered under the light fixture. She sniffed loudly, rubbing her son's shoulder. "If I lost him," she began to whisper. "If I'd lost him."

My mother was stroking the child's hand, her eyes, too, filled with tears. "Don't even think about it," she said. "Don't even imagine it."

But Leela wanted to complete her thought. "If I lost him," she said, "I'd end up with nothing. I only have this one baby. What will I end up with if I lose him?"

My mother glanced at me and I knew for the first time that it was not our perfection, my brother's and mine, that she'd been hoping to duplicate. It was insurance she'd been looking for, and any living child would have sufficed.

SHERYL CALLED HI to me from the sidewalk in front of our house and then to my surprise and delight walked up our driveway. She carried her looseleaf binder and a small paperback book. There was a dark, pilly sweater thrown over her arm.

This was in the early spring, four months or so before that night. It had been a warm day, perhaps the first warm day of the season, and although it was now growing cool, there was still the lingering odor of bright sunlight, the spring smell of fresh dirt. I had brought my Barbie doll out to the front porch, probably because my brother and his friends were somewhere in the house and this was my way of showing my disdain. I had the black dollcase opened at the top of the steps and was choosing a dinner outfit.

Sheryl said as she approached, "How are you?" as if she asked quite regularly.

I must have said something like "Fine."

"This your Barbie?" she asked.

I said yes.

"It's nice." She suddenly sat on the step just below mine and placed her books on her lap. I could see the initials she had written all over her looseleaf binder with black Magic Marker, hers and Rick's. I noticed how the ink had bled a little into the fabric. I could have been glimpsing her garter belt, her diary, the initials seemed so adult and exotic, so indicative of everything I didn't know.

Turning a little, she reached back to my dollcase and gently touched all the tiny dresses and skirts that were hanging there. Her fingers were thin and short and the edges of her nails pressed into her flesh as if she had only recently stopped chewing them. Then she touched the bare feet of the doll.

"She needs shoes," she said.

I told her I was trying to decide which outfit to put on.

Sheryl looked through the clothes again and extracted a pale blue jumper with a white frilly blouse.

"This is cute," she said.

I'd had something more sophisticated in mind, but I was somewhat bewildered by her presence—did she really want to play?—and so I bowed to what I thought was her better judgment.

I slipped off the brown sheath the doll was wearing. (Someday I'll do a study: What's become of that part of my generation who insisted that their Barbie dolls wear underpants and bras? What's become of the rest of us, who dressed her only in what could be seen?)

"Where's she going?" Sheryl asked.

"Out to dinner," I said.

Sheryl held the dress by its little hanger. "On a date?"

I nodded.

"With her boyfriend?"

I said, "Yeah." At that age I was suspicious of any adult, any

teenager, who too willingly joined in my imaginary games. But
Sheryl was good. There was no smirk behind her words.

"Well then," she said, "you want something dressier than this."
She again looked through the clothes and this time extracted a
strapless red dress with a wide gold lamé belt. It was the dress I
had more or less planned to choose from the start.

As I slipped the naked doll into it, Sheryl opened her purse and
began to rummage through it. There was a sound of tumbling
and clicking, plastic and glass.

"Do you have a boyfriend?" she asked me.

I said I didn't.

"Not even anyone you like a little bit?"

I shook my head. I wasn't saying. "Where's your boyfriend?" I
asked her.

She looked up from her bag and glanced toward her house. "He
had to go to the hospital to pick up his mother," she said. "She's
been sick, she's a nutcase, but now she's coming home. For a while
anyway, the weekend. He's got to help out." She lifted her black bag
again and squinted into it. "I guess I won't see him until tomorrow
or something."

I understood: she was bored, friendless, without him. She was
speaking to me merely to pass the time, maybe to keep from having to go home.

I watched her extract a single cigarette and a matchbook from
her bag. She looked at me cautiously but without a word and then
lit up. I watched her draw, her chin raised.

"Are you going steady?" I asked, although I knew.

She said, "Yeah," smoke pouring from her nostrils, and then
lifted her arm to show me Rick's heavy ID bracelet. She turned
her wrist to show me where she'd had a jeweler add an extra catch
so it wouldn't slip over her hand. The inside of her wrist was pale

white, almost blue, marked with red and purple veins. She pulled the bracelet around so the nameplate rested there. We both looked at it. The name was engraved in bold straight lines like Roman numerals.

I leaned over my lap to touch it and was surprised to find it wasn't ice-cold.

"Did he have to ask you?" I said, making plans of my own. "Did you have to wait until he asked you to go steady?"

"He had to ask me," she said. She tuned the bracelet again and then shook her wrist until it fell, just so, over the back of her hand. "But I knew he was going to." She looked at me from under her bangs. "I knew it the minute I met him."

Her perfume reminded me of my father's aftershave. Her eyes were rimmed with smooth black eyeliner that grew, expertly, I thought, thick just over her eyeball and then quickly tapered to a fine, feathery tail that ended about a quarter of an inch beyond the corner of her eye. There was a touch of white powder on her lids.

"How did you know?" I asked.

She held the cigarette between the porch step and her legs and slowly leaned back against the railing. "I just knew," she said. She raised her other hand to brush the bangs from her eyes. The bracelet slid down her arm.

"But how?" I said again. "Who told you?"

Sheryl shrugged and then pulled her lips over her teeth to smile. "No one told me," she said. "I just knew it. In fact, I told him." She looked toward her house again. There were thin short wisps of hair pulled down in front of her ears like sideburns. There was something hard and tense about the set of her jaw. She quickly raised the cigarette. "I told him the very first night we met."

This was marvelous to me: that she knew, that she told him. And more, that she was here telling me.

"What did he say?" I asked her.

She toyed with the corner of her paperback, flipping the pages. "He didn't know," she said. She looked at me. "See, he'd had a lot of girlfriends before me. He didn't think it was going to be any different. He just kind of said, 'Oh yeah?'" She raised her chin, imitating him, then laughed again.

I was still leaning toward her, my Barbie doll all but forgotten. I don't think I'd ever been this close to Sheryl before—certainly not for this long—and I don't know which I took in more eagerly, what she said or how she looked. I remember there were a few pimples on her chin, almost buried beneath the thick makeup, a few flecks of pale pink lipstick on her small mouth. Her cigarette smoke curled toward me, and I breathed deeply.

"What we have," she said, and she may have looked a little sly as she spoke, "is completely different."

"How come?" I asked.

She thought for a moment and then leaned forward, pulling her books up onto her lap, her tight skirt binding her thighs. I saw the flash of her ankle bracelet under her dark stocking: another gift from Rick, another sign of going steady.

"It's just different," she said. She was holding her mouth as if she wanted to grin. "I mean, I'm not like any of those other girls. I've been through a lot of things and so I know more." She seemed to squint at me, perhaps gauging my understanding. "And I'm not afraid of anything," she added. "I'm really not."

I nodded. I saw that she had written their initials on the cover of her paperback as well.

"I'm not even afraid of dying," she told me, the cigarette at her lips. Her tone was pleasant but self-assured. She blew smoke upward into the air. "They showed us movies of these car accidents in school and it didn't even bother me. Even Rick got nervous

when he saw them, but I said, 'So what? Everyone's going to die.'"
She looked at me carefully through the smoke and then sat back
again, letting her head touch the railing. She wore a navy-blue
scarf around her throat. One end was thrown behind her, the other
hung down in front of her bright red shell. Except for a small
bruise just above her scarf, what the Meyer twins had taught us to
recognize as a love bite, her throat was as white as the inside of her
wrist.

"Pretty day," she said softly, looking up at the sky. I looked, too,
ready to follow her anywhere. "Yeah," I said.

And then, still studying the sky, she told me, "My father died
last year."

I don't know when the deaths in other people's lives stop seeming merely inevitable and start becoming a kind of embarrassment.
I know that now I would greet such a statement with a quick consolation and a change of subject, but then I simply said, "I know it."

With her head still back, she turned and once again reached out
to touch the doll dresses, the cigarette burning between her fingers.
"Before that," she said with some disgust, "I didn't know anything.
I thought it was stupid that people you really loved could just die. I
used to think that it would be better if we were all like squirrels or
something so when people died we wouldn't feel so terrible."

She dropped her hand and slowly ran her finger along the edge
of the step. "I didn't know anything," she said.

Then she raised her head and looked at me. Her mouth was
low in her face. There were clumps of mascara in her long lashes.
"Listen," she said. "If you knew everybody you loved was just going to end up disappearing, you'd probably say, Why bother, right?
You'd probably even stop liking people if you knew it wasn't going
to make any difference, they're just going to eventually disappear.
Right?" She leaned closer. I began to understand what my mother

meant when she said that girls who dressed like Sheryl looked tough. There was something tough, even arrogant about her now. "I mean how logical is it," she went on, "for you to love somebody and then they just die, like you never existed? How stupid would it be to keep loving someone who was dead if you were never going to see them again—what do you love, then, air?"

I shrugged and she suddenly sat back, "No you don't," she said impatiently. "You don't end up loving air."

She raised her cigarette again, her elbow resting on the binder. "That's why it wouldn't matter if Rick got killed or something," she went on, cool, even nonchalant. "I guess it would be lonely, but it wouldn't be like I'd never see him again or anything. It would be just like with me and my father. I miss him, but I know I'm going to see him again because I think about him all the time. And you don't keep loving someone who doesn't exist anymore. You can't just stop loving someone because they die. Right?" She suddenly looked at me, demanding a response. "Right?"

"Right," I said softly. I had no idea what she was talking about. "I guess."

She glanced down at her books, ran her finger over the inked initials. "The problem with Rick was nobody loved him enough before me. If he had died, and once he was in a car accident where he could have, he wouldn't have had anyone who still cared about him. He would have just stopped being, like a squirrel or a cat or something. He would have been forgotten about completely. Maybe not right away, but eventually." She picked a piece of tobacco from her tongue, lowering her thick lashes as she did, and then flicked her cigarette, dropping ashes onto our bricks. "His mother has mental problems. Sometimes she even forgets about him now, so what difference would it make to her if he died all of a sudden? She's in her own world. I met her one time." She shook her head.

"And his father has too many problems to ever really think about him. His sisters, too. If he had died before he met me, everybody would have felt bad for a little while and then they would have forgotten about him. Pretty soon it would have been like he'd never been born in the first place. But I wouldn't forget."

We sat silently for a few minutes. My backside was growing cold against the bricks, but I didn't want to go inside.

"Are you getting married?" I asked her.

She shrugged and again looked over her shoulder to her own house before snuffing out her cigarette and tossing it onto our lawn. "I guess so," she said. She leaned back once more, holding an elbow in each palm. She was completely, amazingly, self-possessed. Completely sure. Tough.

"Probably we'll get married," she said. It was clear the subject was not nearly as interesting to her as their immortality. "Maybe in a couple of years. Not that it would make any difference." She glanced at me, but I failed to catch her meaning. "None of that matters to us. You know, getting married and having kids and buying a house. None of that means anything to us."

"How come?" I asked, and she smiled as if she had just proven her point.

"I told you," she said. "I know things. I've been through things. I know all those things that other people think are important come down to nothing. They disappear."

The air had grown chillier, but it was a spring chill, without the bite of winter. Sheryl suddenly arched her back and reached up to touch the teased crown of her hair. There were a thousand things I wanted to ask her: what movies she and Rick went to, what she said to him when he called her on the phone, when they sat together in his car—how she drew such perfect lines across her eyelids.

The death stuff amazed me, but no more than all the rest. It seemed only a part, a profound, important but no less puzzling part of all I would need to know in order to become a teenager. All that I feared I would somehow fail to learn.

Sheryl lifted the Barbie doll from my lap, adjusted her belt and hair, turned to the dollcase to find a pair of little red high heels. I wished she were my sister and I wondered without much hope if she could somehow become my friend. She handed the doll back to me and suggested I wrap a white stole around her bare shoulders.

As I buttoned the tiny fur, I said, "Well, I hope Rick doesn't die."

"Everybody's going to die," she said quickly, and I thought for certain that I'd completely missed her point. Then she smiled, nodding slightly. "But I know what you mean," she said.

She gathered her books into her arms. I watched her walk home: the clink of his bracelet, the gold flash from her ankle, the paperback and looseleaf binder marked with their names. There was something sullen about her walk, a kind of challenge. I saw her toss her hair back over her shoulder before she pulled open the front door, armed and ready, it seemed to me, to battle even the Angel of Death.

What Rick thought of all this I can only guess. I tend to imagine he was somewhat confused but nevertheless thrilled by it all. No one before had ever loved him enough. No one else could have saved him as she would save him. He would find it fantastic, no doubt— the first night they met he had laughed and said, "Oh yeah?" He may even have recognized some of her sources: the love songs of the Shirelles and Shangri-las, the auto accident/undying love poems printed in odd spaces in her teen magazines, the old-fashioned, heaven-saturated Catholicism of her grandmother. But he was a teenager, a troubled one at that; he would not have been able to resist the heady combination of love and sex and death, even if he could never fully understand it.

Because to understand it, he would have had to see her that morning months before they met, when she had looked up from her desk at school, grateful for the distraction of Mrs. Eason, the principal's secretary, coming into the room. He would have to know how idly she had watched as the teacher bent to listen to the old woman and then turned to look her way. He said her name softly, although he was a cold, indifferent young man who never met his students' eyes. He took the exam she'd been working on and said she could finish it when she got back.

The principal at our high school in those days was a chubby, sweet-looking bachelor with an effeminate voice that had aroused no suspicion until years later, when he spoke through a bullhorn trying to quell a student protest. Then his thick lazy drawl, his slight lisp as he said, "Boys and girls," had sounded loudly over the crowd of belligerent students, crossed the playing field and the boulevard and reached the bakery and butcher shop and candy store on the other side, where it lit the rumors that eventually cost him his job.

He could not recall ever having seen Sheryl before, but he spoke to her as if they were friends, his hand on her shoulder as he led her into his office, his large white face unable to conceal his own dread of what he had to say.

The mother had requested that Sheryl be told right away. She didn't want to have to explain it all herself: the heart attack and the car pulled to the side of the road, the police finding him already dead.

Sheryl asked, "How can that be true?" facing him as she had faced me, impatient, demanding a response. And then she began to cry.

The principal drove her home in his own car. On the way, he remembered his own father's death and how just that morning he had thought of the old man and been surprised once again at the clarity with which he recalled his thin bandy legs and his bullet-shaped head and the way he had raised his cupped hand to his bald spot. He glanced at Sheryl's childish profile. It was, he thought, much harder on the young, but there it was. There was no help for it. The man was dead. The tragedy, even now when she still could not begin to comprehend it, was already part of her history. She would learn to accept it as he had learned to accept so many difficult parts of his own.

He thought of telling her this but knew there would be no sense to it right now. Instead, he imagined, he'd call her into his office in another month or two. He could see himself leaning across his desk, speaking softly, or taking the girl down to the cafeteria and gallantly buying her a carton of lemonade. "It's hard to have to learn this so young," he would say. "But loss is what life's all about."

The imagining pleased him as he drove the ten blocks to her house, even relieved some of the pity he felt for her, and his own bloated sense of sadness.

Sitting beside him, Sheryl was at first stunned by his kindness. To think that she was riding alone with the principal in his own car. To think he had called her by her first name and let her briefly cry in his arms. The peculiarity of it made what he had told her even more unreal. She found herself wondering why he wasn't married, if he had a girlfriend or spent countless weekday evenings calling women he had just met, trying not to sound too anxious when he asked to see them once more. She wondered who would be called if, driving this very car, he pulled to the side of the road and died. She wondered if anyone loved him.

The neighborhood at this hour had a different life and this, too, made the morning seem dreamlike. There were pillows and blankets being aired from upstairs windows and crowds of clothes hanging on nearly every line. She saw a woman unloading grocery bags from her car, a large cookie stuck in her mouth and a child on her hip. Another two talking in the middle of the sidewalk, one with a baby carriage that she rocked back and forth as she spoke. They passed Angie's house, where it looked as though no one was home, and a house where she sometimes baby-sat, an empty playpen in its driveway.

At this hour there were only women in the neighborhood, as if somewhere a war still raged, and Sheryl saw that every one of them was unaware that what was ordinary about the day had been arrested and forever transformed. This was the day her father died.

She began to whimper, and the principal, who was by now thinking of the teacher's meeting he would be late for, whispered, "I know, honey," reminding her again of his kindness.

She had said, "How can that be true?" because she could still see him, hear his voice. And worse, because she still loved him. She had not been good; she had fought with him about her makeup and her hair. She had accused him just the other day of disapproving of everyone and everything, of wanting her to be lonely, but she loved him. And wouldn't her love stop or change, begin even now slowly to disappear, if what the principal had told her was true?

It was not logical, she thought, for it to be so pointless. He was not just anyone who had died in the middle of an ordinary morning. He was her own father. He was loved.

She saw the police car at the curb when they approached the house, and closed her eyes, refusing to believe it. Because how could the daily wash and the grocery shopping and the test that was still unfinished back at school, Mrs. Eason and the principal and the toddler she sometimes minded all continue to matter when love could so quickly be made pointless? When love always, finally, would have to be dismantled and unraveled, put away and forgotten because it couldn't keep its own object from forever leaving the earth.

Unluckily, as the neighborhood women later put it, just minutes before the principal arrived with Sheryl, another policeman had pulled her father's car into her driveway, returning it to the family. When Sheryl saw it there, she pushed wildly at the car door and then ran up the steps to her house. She seemed to be laughing and the women all up and down the block could hear her call to her father as she entered.

In order to even begin to understand, Rick would have to imagine the triumph in her voice that morning, when she had believed that by the mere force of her love she had saved him.

Their nights together always began with the others in the parking lot outside the bowling alley or in the schoolyard. I imagine she was quiet then. She would watch from under her bangs as the boys bragged and joked. She would watch Rick with only the slightest smile as he stepped away from her to illustrate some story. He would raise his arms, lifting the hem of his jacket, and at the punchline wriggle his backside. The other boys would notice her squinting through her cigarette smoke, smiling slightly, her eyes on his tight pants, and they would remark to themselves, although not in so many words: Still waters run deep.

His joke told, his status among them confirmed, Rick would step back to where she leaned against his car and once again pull her under his arm. She would hold his belt, and the homely boys, or those simply less lucky in love, the virgins, the chronic masturbators, would have to remind themselves that Sheryl was not really all that great-looking, lest they weep with envy. When the hour came for the two of them to drive off alone together, the boys would nod coolly, say, "See ya." They would turn to the remaining girls with new interest. Turn especially and with the greatest charm to those known as the tramps among them.

Alone, Sheryl and Rick would simply drive for a while, Sheryl sitting close to him in the wide front seat, her hand on his thigh. Rick with his arm around her. Slowly, she would begin to tell him things, about his friends or his family, about the meaning of the songs that came on the radio, speaking with that same assurance she had shown me, the assurance that she had been through more than any of them, that she knew more.

"Larry really likes that girl he's dating," she might tell him. "He just won't admit it because she's so heavy. He's afraid you guys will make fun of him."

"No," Rick would say. "He's using her. He's just getting laid. He told me himself."

Sheryl would nod. "Just wait and see. See what he gives her for Christmas."

He would learn to depend on her and the way she looked at things. He would begin to believe she knew more than anyone.

During that summer when they first met, through the fall they spent together, again in the spring as soon as the ground had begun to dry and that part of the summer they had before she went away, they would end their nights in the park on the other side of town. It was a long, narrow piece of land fronting on the busy, brightly lit boulevard but surrounded on its farthest end by dim streets lined with small homes. On the boulevard side there were swings and slides, basketball courts, and in summer a concrete wading pool, but the back half was given over to a baseball diamond, a picnic area and, on a hill that marked the end of the property, a sparse approximation of a wood.

Seven or eight years later, when I was Sheryl's age, this was the place to buy and use drugs, to drink sweet apple wine or sangria from leather wineskins, pretending you were at Woodstock, but then, when the park still closed at dusk, it was a place where only the most serious couples went to make love.

The trick in Sheryl's day was to find an inconspicuous spot to leave your car, somewhere along one of the side streets, far enough from the park itself to avoid suspicion but not so far that you could be seen by too many people as you walked, with a brown paper bag filled with Cokes and a bottle of rum, toward the lowest part of the fence.

Once over the fence, you would only have to choose your niche among the trees. A police cruiser would pass through each night at about twelve or one, but it would never leave the road that circled the baseball diamond and so it was easy enough to avoid its headlights.

Sheryl and Rick would sit down together on a sloping bit of dirt and grass. Rick would open the bottles of Coke, pour out half, open the flask bottle of rum. In the semidarkness (there were two or three tall night lights in the park, some small bit of light from the surrounding streets), he would match the lips of the two bottles carefully, pour the rum with a precise and steady hand. ("This is what my old man does for a living," he told her. "Pours piss and blood from one bottle to another.") They would sit shoulder to shoulder, their knees raised, the bottles in their hands.

She might tell him then: "I used to think it was stupid that people you really loved could just die . . ."

Moving her hand across the dirt and the grass, she might say, "If one of us died."

He would tell her about the car accident he had been in before he met her. An older friend had been driving. They had cut school and smoked some reefer. They had been drinking all day. At about nine o'clock that night, in a town not far away—his friend had been looking for the house of some girl he knew—they turned a corner and hit a parked car. Neither of them knew how or why. They both might have been asleep. They were laughing when they crawled out, one through a window, one through a back door. The engine was nearly in the front seat. Rick's father said that if they'd hit a tree or a pole, something that couldn't have rolled with the impact as the car did, they both would have been killed. His father had said it would have served them right.

Sheryl would whisper, "Before me, you would have been forgotten."

Or perhaps by then she would no longer have to say it. By then, he would understand it himself, even as he told her the story, as he remembered his father's tired, angry voice, his mother's dazed indifference. If he had died then, before he met her, who would have loved him enough to make his disappearance from the earth illogical?

Perhaps by then he understood only that when she spoke of dying he should turn to her, loosen the scarf at her throat or her waist, gently push her back onto the grass.

He lay beside her, his cheek to the cool ground, his arm across her waist. She studied the sky, speaking softly and with that same sure tone. Beyond her were the two empty Coke bottles, his wallet, opened flat, the ripped silver paper from the condom, the circle of her scarf. He watched the line of her profile, the shadowy movement of her dark lashes as she whispered to him, her face to the sky. The police headlights passed through the trees, but they hardly made her pause; she was afraid of nothing in that world that seemed only, even superfluously, to begin at the end of these woods. Speaking softly but with that same assurance, she would name for him all the things that didn't matter to them, that didn't have to matter to them, and it seemed to him that she started at the foot of those woods and worked outward, dismissing, obliterating, the entire world: not friends, she told him, not family, not school, not getting older or getting married or finding a job. Not car accidents or hospitals, not any kind of luck, good or bad, not dying.

She turned to him and even in the darkness he saw that same brightness in her eyes, a hard, challenging gleam. Only they mattered. They loved each other. It would not be logical for love to bring them to anything else. And later, when she sat up, laughing, draping her scarf over her bare shoulders like a shawl, he reminded himself that she knew things no one else seemed to know.

IN A TOWN not far from ours, there was a school run by the Salvation Army or the Baptists and called, blatantly enough, the Wayside School. For troubled girls, my mother would tell me as we drove past, for girls in trouble. (The irony of it was never lost upon her: all her prayers and all her formulas for pregnancy coming to nothing while mere children were conceiving, casually, inadvertently, in parking lots and playgrounds.) It was surrounded by a high stockade fence so that only its green and silver sign was visible from the road, and the driveway that led into it was blocked by an iron gate. I never saw the school buildings themselves, never knew anyone who went there, but each Christmas one of the classes in our own school would draw Wayside as its place to send Christmas packages. Draw it from a field that included the children's ward at the nearby mental hospital, a city prison, a Catholic orphanage and innumerable nursing homes. The girls at Wayside, the class would be told each year, would appreciate perfume, hand cream, small stuffed animals and dusting powder. Each year the class was asked not to enclose notes, names or addresses with their gifts.

In college, I met a girl who had grown up just a few blocks from the school. She told me about the occasional incident when one of the "students" tried to bolt, running wild and confused (and sometimes, too appropriately, barefoot) through their neighborhood or down the main street. Once, she and some of her girlfriends—they couldn't have been more than nine or ten at the time—took a ladder from a set of bunk beds and carried it through the backyard of a neighbor and across a gully to some obscure part of the school's high fence. It had been about dusk on a summer evening and they had taken turns climbing up. They stood on tiptoe, on the top rung, gripping the points of the fence's wooden stakes, but what they saw made the effort worthwhile: a half dozen teenage girls, most of them pregnant, listlessly tossing a beach ball across a lush green lawn.

Eventually, one of the teenagers noticed the children, or perhaps one of the children grew brave enough to call out, and the entire group moved toward the fence. At first they exchanged information politely, with some of the cautious fascination of Martian to Earthling. "Hello!" they said. "Where did you come from?" The unwed mothers, with their hands on their hips and their bangs in their eyes, laughed each time one of the children stepped down and another head appeared. It must have been a kind of puppet show for them. "And what's your name?" they'd ask each new face. "And what kind of house do you live in?" The children themselves turning to look down—"What? What?"—taking instructions from the invisible chorus below.

When some kind of rapport had been established, the teenagers asked for cigarettes. Of course the children had none, but yes, they had parents who smoked. Their parents would never miss one pack, the pregnant girls assured them. (And here our school officials should be commended for their foresight. What might have happened to my own classmates had they included their names and addresses when they wrapped their two cans of hairspray and card of bobby pins in Christmas paper? What requests might they have received from the Wayside girls in return: Go into your parents' room while they are sleeping. Remove the following from your fathers' handkerchief drawer . . .)

Two of the children said, almost immediately, "I'll be right back." The others said, "We'll bring you some tomorrow." And magazines, the girls said, good magazines like *Modern Romance, 16, True.* Could they ever get them magazines? The children conferred. One climbed the ladder to say her sister read *16* and *Teen Screen.* She was forced down by the breathless return of the others, who carried packs of Camels and Pall Malls.

And makeup, the unwed mothers asked. Could they maybe bring them some makeup? But suddenly one of them said, "Beat it," and the teenagers scrambled. The children crouched at the foot of the fence, mouthing to each other, "Someone's coming."

When they climbed the ladder again, after night had fallen, they saw only the yellow lights of the distant dormitory windows and the bloated shadows of the girls who passed behind them.

The next morning, deprived of their ladder by an irate mother, the children heaved three issues of *Teen Screen* over the fence and were startled to hear the voice of some woman—a teacher or warden or nurse—warn them that she would call the police if they tried that again.

I could draw on my own experience to imagine how Sheryl felt in the months before that night, draw detail and scene from what I remember of my own brief pregnancy and from all the awkward and untimely pregnancies of my friends, but I fear something would be lost. Unwed mothers at that time, at the time Sheryl joined their ranks, were a specific group; they fell somewhere between criminals and patients and, like criminals and patients, they were prescribed an exact and fortifying treatment: They were made to disappear.

So I would have to add to my own memories of my own troublesome pregnancy not merely some sense of shame and a bit more drama but also a different kind of fear: when her period didn't come (this would have been late spring, not very long after she had stopped to talk to me), when she found herself dizzy with nausea every morning, unable to eat her cereal (she would get up before her mother and grandmother, pour a bit of milk and a few crumbs of corn flakes into a bowl and leave it unwashed in the kitchen sink), when she had to keep herself from imagining the taste and the smell of the eggs, the frozen green beans, the jars of peanut butter she rang up on her register and packed into brown paper bags.

I would have to add to my own experience a kind of fear that another fifteen years would make obsolete: the fear of a criminal with the police at the windows and doors, of a patient trapped in some unrelenting illness.

If she was pregnant, an unwed mother, she would have to be sent away. In all her theories of love and dying and keeping one another alive, in all her certainty, she could not have anticipated this simple, insurmountable problem: if she was pregnant, she might never see him again.

Another month passed. Another period failed to begin. Her breasts felt tender, her stomach was no longer quite so taut between the protruding bones of her hips. Leaning with him against his car, listening to them all talk and laugh, watching some of the boys and some of the girls who had not yet become lovers move toward one another, she might have wanted to beg for silence. Please, just everyone be quiet. Her cigarettes were beginning to make her feel sick. She would have to pretend to sip from her can of beer, though the smell alone was enough to send her reeling. Rick, beside her, his arm heavy on her shoulders, would at moments seem a stranger, as the healthy always seem strange and uncaring to those who are ill. She would have to slip her fingers through his belt loop, pull him closer to her, rest her nose and her lips on the arm of his cool leather jacket. Closing her eyes against the dim parking-lot lights and the childish sound of their voices, she would have to breathe him in, the odor of the leather, of his aftershave and, indistinguishable from it, her own perfume, of the summer night, sun-warmed parking lot and litter.

Later, she held the bag of Coke and rum as he climbed the jingling chain-link fence. She followed him, lowering the bag over the top, pausing at the top herself to remember how her hands, even her legs, had shaken the first time she had made this awkward turn, from the outside of the fence to the inside. Making it easily now, her fingers knowing just how lightly to grip the thin wire, her toes finding just the right spaces even in the dark. Rick touched her legs as soon as he could reach them. Took hold of her hips with both hands.

At some point she must have considered telling him. She must have imagined their conversation. They would be lying together on their hill or sitting side by side like children, their knees raised, the bottles of Coke in their hands.

"Rick, what if I got pregnant?"

"You won't. We're careful."

"But what if?"

A shrug, but his eyes would be far away. "We'd get married."

"How?"

"What do you mean, how? I don't know. You get a license."

"And move in with my mother?"

Another shrug.

"Or your father?"

"You could get an abortion."

"How?"

"I don't know. I'd have to find out." Laughing, "I could ask my old man to do it. You're not going to get pregnant."

She would have to whisper, "Not that it would matter. It wouldn't matter anyway." But still he would see she had been wrong; it wasn't just them. There was also family and school, getting a job and getting older. There was all that long life that had become for her since the day her father died a sentence, a burden. There was all that long life, all those years until she would see him again, years of family and friends and school and getting a job and getting older—years that would be double and triple, four, even five, times the years she had already lived—and none of her promises, none of her assurances, could shorten them or lighten their load or, as she had wanted to do, obliterate them completely. They loved each other and they would continue to love each other, as they did on those dark nights when they seemed alone in the world, even after one of them died, but what until then? How would they get through all the years until then?

She stretched beside him on the damp ground, aware of the tenderness in her breasts, the weeks and days since her last period, a certain tightness at her waist. She began at the edge of the woods and worked outward: not this, not this, nothing else mattered.

When she went into her mother's room that morning, she knew what she was setting in motion. Other girls in her school had suddenly disappeared. One, when Sheryl was a freshman, had been banned from the school, actually turned away from her homeroom, because her pregnancy had become too obvious to ignore. She knew what would happen, and only the speed of it all startled her.

While her mother rose and immediately went to the phone, Sheryl got up off her knees and sat carefully on the edge of the bed. The nausea made her weak, made her limbs feel thick and sodden. The sound of the children's voices as they came through the open windows made her want to put her hands to her ears. Her mother spoke into the phone, and Sheryl, in her thin summer pajamas, in the warm blue room, trembled. Trembled once to think that the night before, when he'd said from the bottom of the steps, "I'll meet you tomorrow after work," and then turned and walked toward his car, was the last time in her life she would ever see him. Trembled to remember the morning she had come downstairs into the kitchen where her father was taking a final gulp of coffee before he kissed her mother and then patted her just-teased hair to say, "So long, sleepy-head." The last time in her life she would ever see him.

I must add to my own memories of my own pregnancy—for mine was fifteen years later and far too early in my marriage to be allowed to come to term—her strange assurance: It would not be forever. It wasn't possible that people who loved each other could be apart forever.

IN THE DAYS that followed the fight, while our fathers moved together to share their wounds and rehearse their triumph, while we
children stepped back from the sidewalks and the streets to make
way for them—suspending our present, you might say, while they
recalled some part of their past—our mothers watched Sheryl's
house as if they knew something. Passing behind their own windows, their own summer screens, they paused, bent a little, glanced
out. Each morning they took their coffee to the living room and
drank it standing in the shaft of white sunlight that came through
their front door. At night they kept vigil in unlit rooms. We would
discover them quite by accident when we flipped a light switch: they
would be flattened against the wall beside a drawn shade or crouched
by a window, one finger still caught in the slat of a blind. Coming
upon them, we would jump more than necessary, yell, "Ah!" or
"Yikes!" the way startled people did on television. Our mothers
would hiss, "Turn if off," as if they feared someone else might hear.

Joining them in the darkness, we too would peer into the

street, the white pools of lamplight and the pale gray stripes of sidewalk and driveway, the yellow glow of our neighbors' windows.
Under the moon and the stars, there were identical rooftops and
chimneys and TV antennas, no minarets or onion domes, and the
trees that caught and muffled the lamplight were ordinary oak and
maple. A car would pass by in its familiar hushing sound and stop
as it should at the stop sign (the headlights, for one moment, making the sign flash black and silver) and then carefully go on. We
would lean against our mothers, hear their breaths, smell the summer dust on the windows and the blinds. Even from our second-
story vantage point there was nothing exotic or unusual about the
scene. Except the night. And in those days that followed the fight,
the night brought to our street as well what it more famously brings
to foreign cities and forests of pine. Between the soft lamplight and
room light there were dark places (we now knew) where lovers
threw back their heads and either grinned at the stars or howled
with longing. There was the black flash of uncertainty, the wet-eyed
smile of stealthy chance. The sound, behind the ordinary sound of a
cough or a car or of dishes tumbling in a sink full of water, of something receding, the low roll and tumble of something we had not
yet even imagined as it approached.

We felt our mothers draw their breath as another car went by.
We felt them slowly ease again into a kind of waiting. Standing
beside them, we would stare down into the street in dull amazement, wondering at our fathers, who passed below, even lingered.

Early one evening during these days that followed the fight, Mrs.
Carpenter came up from the basement where she and her family
lived to glance once more toward Sheryl's house. Her husband
was in the driveway polishing his car, and she waved to him but

he had already turned his attention to someone (my father) across
the street. She was then free to look steadily over her own driveway,
and the Rossis', toward Sheryl's house. That afternoon she had seen,
as we children had seen, as all our mothers had seen from behind
their windows and doors (a laundry basket on the chair beside them
or one hand held under a dripping spoon), an unmarked police car
pull into Sheryl's driveway and a weary plainclothes policeman
climb her steps. She had seen, as all our mothers had seen, Sheryl's
mother come to the door and let him in, and although she had to
hurry back down to the basement where the Carpenters more or
less lived to turn off the running water, she was again at her window when the door opened and closed and the car pulled out of the
drive. Her phone had rung then, phones all up and down the street
had begun ringing, but no one could say what it meant. Mrs. Carpenter learned only that Sheryl's mother wore a bandage on her
wrist—she hadn't seen it herself—and that she didn't look all that
bad, considering. It was hardly enough.

She left her side door and climbed the two steps into her upstairs kitchen. It was yellow and white, spotless because it was,
for the most part, unused. The Carpenters, Mr. and Mrs., Billy,
Wayne and Little Alice, spent most of their waking hours in their
basement, and it probably says more about us than them that this
never really struck anyone as queer or unusual. It was a nice basement, after all, with wall-to-wall carpeting and pine paneling and
a television built right into the wall. There was even a kitchenette,
a dining table, a bath with a stall shower. There were curtains on
the tiny windows and crushed-velvet throw pillows on the sofa and
the chairs, and these had been bought specifically for the basement, not merely demoted there after long and faithful service in
the living room. There was the requisite bar with padded swirling
stools and a ceramic drunk holding onto a lamppost, even a small

workshop behind the finished part where Mr. Carpenter could pound nails and the boys could shoot their pellet guns. It was, by neighborhood consensus, the finished basement of all finished basements, and if a bomb wiped away all our homes, the Carpenters, it was agreed, would hardly notice the loss. This, however, was not what they were practicing for.

The Carpenters lived in their basement because the rest of their house was too beautiful to bear. At least this is what the women who had seen it (none of us children ever got beyond a glance into the upstairs kitchen) reported on their return. The first time Mrs. Carpenter gave her the full, shoeless tour, my mother came home holding her heart and saying there was nothing else like it in the world. The shine on the dining room table was blinding. The living room was all white and gold. The carpet, she said, felt like fur laid over clouds. There were flowers pressed in glass all up and down the staircase. The children's two bedrooms were papered and paneled and full of shining brass fixtures, like something you'd see on a yacht. The master bedroom was a sultan's palace, deep green and pink and silver with drapes hanging where there weren't even windows. Not a thing out of place, not a thing that didn't match. A gold swan spouting water in the bathroom sink, its wings Hot and Cold.

Upon her return from what seemed to us the enchanted, mist-shrouded heights—the upstairs part of the Carpenters' house—my mother threatened to break my brother's arm if he didn't learn to hang up his coat, and she told me that the state of my dresser drawers constituted the biggest disappointment of her life. She claimed our house, too, had once been lovely and seemed to indicate that its decline began only with our birth. At dinner, she threw a boiled potato at my father's head when he said he much preferred the lived-in look.

While the men gathered at the foot of our driveway that evening of the same day the police car pulled into Sheryl's drive, Mrs. Carpenter surveyed her kitchen, perhaps hoping the sight of it—the perfect gossamer curtains, the bright pans hanging on the wall, the teapot filled with silk flowers—would cool her curiosity, expand her patience. She may have briefly considered calling my mother again, or Mrs. Rossi, just to see if they'd heard anything, but the husbands were home by now and it would be difficult to talk. And they had already talked all afternoon.

She walked through her kitchen and into her dining room. Even in the fading summer light, the waxed rectangular table shone like a black lake and the two gold candlesticks were reflected in it like tapers in a dark room. In one shadowy corner was the china cabinet, and behind the glass, looking a little ghostly, the floral patterned plates she had taken downstairs and washed carefully every other month since her wedding fifteen years before but had never, according to neighborhood legend, actually used. On the back of each plate, she knew, it said in small red letters: *Made in Occupied Japan*, but she couldn't remember when the phrase had begun to seem quaint, something from a time surprisingly long past. Her youth, perhaps.

Mrs. Carpenter was not, could not have been, a naturally melancholy person or else she surely would have recognized long before this that her lovely rooms would wear and grow old despite her, but the silence that seemed to have been left in the wake of his cry, that night, made her more aware than usual of the weight of each hour. Like nearly all our mothers, Mrs. Carpenter had set her life on her marriage and her home and her children—if they go well, all goes well—and so she sometimes, especially in the early evening or late in the afternoon when no work presented itself, had the bored, distracted air of someone simply waiting to see how things turn out.

Something Sheryl's mother had already seen, she knew. For surely the premature conclusion that her husband's death and her daughter's pregnancy had brought to Sheryl's mother's career as a housewife was for Mrs. Carpenter and all the other mothers a glimpse into the future, a report from the uncharted frontier that their daily lives were slowly but inexorably moving them toward.

Mrs. Carpenter walked into her living room, the thick pale carpeting soft under her feet, even cool. Through the open front door (and if nothing else, air was allowed to circulate freely through this house) came the men's laughter. It had become a familiar sound during those days that followed the fight, as common as the crickets and passing cars. She stood at the door and watched them. Mr. Rossi was just crossing to join them. Little Jake, hunched over his bicycle, his large head rolling, turned up our driveway. She saw my mother on our porch and considered going over to speak with her, but the clutch of men made her hesitate.

She turned again into the room. The television was on downstairs and the running and stopping rhythm of its voice reached her through the carpet. Her curiosity was like a thirst. She sat down in a small chair that even in this house, where everything above the ground was ornamental, seemed ridiculous in its impracticality. Its delicate cherry legs were tapered to the width of dimes and its small seat and back, the size of handmirrors, were pure white, threaded with a touch of gold. Even in the store where she had bought it, she refused to sit in it, telling the salesman, "Oh, it's not for sitting," as if she were the type of woman who could squander chairs, couches, whole rooms of her house.

A bead of perspiration ran down her spine and she arched her back a little more to keep the print of her shift (it was what we then called a muumuu) from touching the fine material.

She was not a tragic figure. She had been fortunate most of her life, healthy and well liked. She loved her husband (although no longer in a way there merited a sultan's palace of deep green and pink and silver—a square serviceable room would have done, a dark plaid, well worn), and she will only occasionally be disappointed by her children: by Billy's sloppy wife and Wayne's brief years as an underground (it's in the blood) city poet, by Little Alice's half-hearted ambition to "do hair." She was not foolish, either. Her pride in her small rooms, her rigorous house rules that no shoes should touch her carpet, no child spend more than ten waking minutes in his bedroom, no guest go unescorted, were merely part of a brave and determined effort to preserve what she knew of Beauty from the ravages of drink-spilling and ash-dropping Time. More artist than eccentric, then. But at this moment, sitting as she is in her tiny chair, her back arched, her ankles crossed, her light brown hair, which she wears above her ears, puffed out and turned under like a buttermilk biscuit, she does seem somewhat pathetic. And it might merely have been the hand of some benevolent being, as concerned with order and perfection as she, that set the telephone ringing then.

It was Sheryl's mother. Her voice was both shy and determined. She was calling, she said, because she was going to be leaving town in the morning, but she would like Billy Carpenter to continue cutting her lawn—what was left of it—while she was away. She wasn't sure how long she'd be gone. She would mail him his check from Ohio.

Mrs. Carpenter nodded like a professional. She said of course Billy would do it. Of course she would tell him. And then she added, her curiosity indistinguishable from what was, to her credit, true concern. "Ann"—a pause that said, I don't know if I should be asking this, I certainly don't want to pry—"is everything all right?"

If you want to see how far we have come from the cave and the woods, from the lonely and dangerous days of the prairie or the plain, witness the reaction of a modern suburban family, nearly ready for bed, when the doorbell rings or the door is rattled. They will stop where they stand, or sit bolt upright in their beds, as if a streak of pure lightning has passed through the house. Eyes wide, voices fearful, they will whisper to one another, "There's someone at the door," in a way that might make you believe they have always feared and anticipated this moment—that they have spent their lives being stalked.

The doorbell rings at midnight and the household stops short in its nightly primordial ritual of curling into itself, reverses it. Knows the news can't be good. It lines up according to size and age and sex, as if for some final reckoning, and heads down the stairs. The patriarch, the matriarch, the strongest and biggest and first to marry, raises a trembling hand and, with the very courage needed to be born, unlocks the door.

Only once, and not again until my brother and I were teenagers with our own Standard Time, had our doorbell rung so late, and that was the night Mr. Murphy's wife died. He was a distant neighbor, barely known to us, although my mother occasionally talked with his wife when they met at the mailbox. He appeared at our door with a little girl, his daughter, one cold night just as my parents were getting ready for bed and told them when they invited him into the kitchen, "Helen passed away at eight o'clock," as if he regretted the pain this news would cause them. Before my father could ask, "Who's Helen?" Mr. Murphy turned to my mother, "You were a friend of hers," his voice more certain than questioning.

Both my parents were in a modest state of undress, beltless, half-buttoned, their faces freshly washed, and there was still some remnant of fear and confusion in my mother's eyes. "I knew her," she said. But then she added, perhaps because she saw something pass over the man's florid face, "She was from Massachusetts."

"Quincy," he said. He raised the little girl's hand, bare in his gloved one. "She told me you knew her." He glanced at my brother and me as we stood together in the kitchen doorway. He seemed pleased to discover my parents had children as well. Then he turned to my father. "You know how it is," he said. "You're at work all day. You never really know who's who in the neighborhood. I knew Helen had plenty of girlfriends. She was always telling me this one said that and that one said this." He shrugged. "You know how it is. You don't really listen."

He touched his free hand to his forehead and paused for a moment, as if he were about to begin a lengthy explanation. "When I got home tonight," he said, "I didn't know what I was supposed to do next." He indicated the child again. She was a homely little thing with those dark, weary circles under her eyes that can make a four-year-old look like a dissipated, hung-over adult. "So I take her outside and I ask her, 'Where do Mommy's girlfriends live?'" He pointed to our refrigerator. "I say to her, 'Over there?' and she says, 'Yeah.'" He pointed to our kitchen sink. "I say, 'How about that house over there?' She says yeah again." He smiled in amazement. He had filled our kitchen with a musty, unwashed smell. "The little girl tells me yeah at every house," he said. "Every single block, she tells me yeah. That's how many friends Helen has."

And then he began to cry, a thick, stocky stranger with short arms. The child hid herself behind his thigh as if she had known this was coming (and, indeed, we later learned that he had done exactly the same in each house he visited). My parents, still looking innocent and fuzzy in the bright colorful kitchen, reached out to touch him briefly here and there, on the shoulder and the arm. They made odd, soothing, inarticulate sounds, sounds that might

have been made before language, when our dumb and curious an-
cestors tried to coax into their hands whatever night creature had
found its way to their fire and their light.

"Here now," my mother said. "Now, now."

The man drew in long, painful breaths. In the weeks that followed, we would see him wandering with the child, drifting in
and out of the butcher shop and the candy store, the supermarket
where our mothers shopped, until the sight of him became so familiar we hardly noticed when he no longer appeared. "And now
I can't tell her," he sobbed. "I can't tell her I've met all her girlfriends."

When Mrs. Carpenter rang our bell, the night of the same day
the police car had pulled into Sheryl's drive, my mother had just
filled the tub, preparing for their nightly ritual. My father was waiting for her in their room. Sitting up in my bed, I heard her open the
bathroom door and run lightly across the hall. "There's someone at
the door," she called in a loud, panicked whisper. I looked toward
my open window, where the trees were silent and thick with hu-
midity. I heard my father stepping back into his pants.

Mrs. Carpenter was still in her Hawaiian print muumuu, although she had one curler in her hair, just above her forehead. She
seemed startled to see all four of us.

"Oh," she said. "I saw your light." She looked beyond my father
to meet my mother's eye. "I thought you were still up."

"Is anything wrong?" my mother asked, but already I could see
some other communication passing between them. Mrs. Carpenter's eyes were full of meaning. "I wanted to talk to you about
something," she said.

My father stepped back to let her in, his every movement showing controlled impatience. "Neither rain nor sleet nor snow," she
said. "Nor dark of night." He shooed my brother and me back up

the stairs and then turned to tell the women, "We'll leave you to your discussions."

My mother said she'd be up in a little while. Mrs. Carpenter said, "Good night." I could tell they were both glad to be rid of us.

From my bed, I heard the tea kettle whistle briefly. I heard the two women's voices, soft and indistinguishable. Not so much conspirators' voices as the hushed, amazed and nervous voices of two who had managed to drag something frightful and extraordinary, some part of the dark and populated night, into our ordinary kitchen light.

They stayed up very late. I heard the kettle whistle once again, and I fell asleep listening to the wordless rush of their voices.

In the morning, my mother at first refused to get out of bed and then came into the kitchen looking unhappy and exhausted. She sighed as she made her coffee and sighed again as she lit her first cigarette. I asked her what Mrs. Carpenter had wanted. She looked at me through half-closed eyes, deciding something, and then said, "None of your business." She went to the window, which looked only into our backyard. I heard her say a disgusted and indifferent "Tch" as she gazed out. Once or twice she shook her head and shrugged her shoulders.

At Diane Rossi's house, I put my hands to the screen door and saw Mrs. Carpenter sitting with Mrs. Rossi at the kitchen table. I heard Mrs. Rossi say something odd and poetic, or at least something overblown and incomprehensible, something like "Tragedy completes all romance," before I interrupted her by ringing the bell. She and Mrs. Carpenter looked at me, and at Diane when she had joined me, much the same way my mother had: not with the proprietary air of the men the night before, but with a sad, cautious assessment, as if they had learned overnight that one of us was a traitor or an alien spy. As if, it occurs to me now, they had only begun to learn that while their love had been sufficient to form us, it would not necessarily keep us alive.

Outside, the sun was bright and hot on the sidewalk and the leaves. I sniffed the air, as if to catch some scent of whatever it was that had happened. Half expecting to smell some trace of Mr. Murphy's fleshy, death-touched odor. Wordlessly, Diane and I strolled past Sheryl's house. The shades were drawn and the tire marks still fresh and violent.

I turned just in time to see my mother stepping through Mrs. Evers's side door.

ON THE MORNING after the fight, I left Leela and my mother and little Jake in our kitchen and stepped outside, where Diane Rossi, Georgie Evers and the Meyer twins were already searching the sidewalk and street in front of Sheryl's house. I knew precisely what they were looking for, and without comment I joined them. In each of our basements and attics, in grimy shoeboxes and old footlockers, in paper bags as limp as cloth, our fathers, we knew, had iron crosses and silver swastikas, tarnished medals marked with bright red suns, heavy foreign coins and black-and-white postcards fading to yellow and brown, and what we searched for that morning was in some way our own version of those souvenirs: mementos of a battle, a night of high drama we were not likely to see again.

As we searched, we discussed what had happened to Sheryl.

Diane said, "They got married secretly, her and her boyfriend. And when her mother found out, she sent her away."

"To Ohio," Georgie said. He crouched to touch a piece of mica that gleamed up from the road. He already held a small shard of black glass. I held another.

"They didn't get married," one of the Meyer twins said, his voice full of scorn. "She's going to have a baby."

"Yeah," the other said. Both of them had long, thin, freckled faces and only the slightest brown fuzz of a crew cut. Their voices, too, were identical. "She's pregnant," he said.

The word alone startled us.

We were silent for a moment and then, together, Diane, Georgie and I said, "We know that," although I'm not sure any of us knew it with such certainty until then. The night before, parents all up and down the block had offered their children short, contingency courses in the birds and the bees, just as my mother had done for me and apparently with as much detail and tact. They were of that generation who spelled the words they couldn't speak and followed strict rules regarding what could be discussed in mixed company, so this morning, we, their children, were more confused than ever about just what was involved.

We studied the tire tracks on the grass by the curb and then crossed the sidewalk and stepped only one inch at a time onto Sheryl's torn lawn. We were all thinking about sex.

"But they got married, too," Diane finally added.

"No they didn't," the Meyer twins told her.

She paused and squinted at them. "Yesss," she said. "My mother told me."

They stuck out their chins. "Nooo," they answered. "Your mother's wrong."

She put her hands on her hips. "How could she have a baby if they weren't married?"

The Meyer twins stopped in their tracks and then slowly staggered backward, their hands on their stomachs, their mouths wide open. Then they threw their arms around one another and whooped with laughter.

Georgie and I moved closer to Diane. We knew she had made a terrible mistake, but we knew our own parents, in explaining Sheryl's dilemma, had said an awful lot about marriage as well. ("When people get married," my own mother had begun, "they do what Sheryl did . . ." as if it were Sheryl herself who had established the trend.)

"Don't you know anything?" Mickey Meyer asked, still holding his stomach but bending now, as if her stupidity had given him appendicitis.

"How old are you?" Ricky cried. "Two or something? You don't have to be married to have a baby, dope."

"Yes you do," she said weakly. She turned to me, "Right?"

Wanting to stay on her side but fairly certain she was wrong, I merely shrugged. This spun Mickey and Ricky around with delight.

"Two idiots!" they cried. I saw Mrs. Rossi glance out her window and I told them to hush. "I know you don't have to be married," I told them.

"You just have to go to sleep with someone," Georgie suddenly added. "That's all."

But the Meyer twins were too delighted with our ignorance to let it go at that. "Oh yeah, sure," Mickey said. He folded his hands under his cheek, closed his eyes and pretended to snore— "gnaa-shew, gnaa-shew"—then he opened his eyes and said in a high-pitched voice, "Uh-oh, I'm going to have a baby."

Ricky threw himself on the edge of Sheryl's lawn and rocked with laughter, touching his shoulder to one of the ripped places on the grass. His own marriage in another ten years' time would be to a girl whom everyone, including his parents, had believed to be Italian until a prenuptial barbecue in the Meyers' backyard had filled our street with cries of "*Mira, mira*," and the Meyers' lawn chairs with three out of five grandparents who were definitely not white.

"You better take No-Doz," he told us now. In another ten years' time he would leave his parents and their house for good—choosing to be dead to them, as his mother put it to mine, rather than give up the love of his mongrel girl.

Georgie looked crestfallen and I, too, was confused. We had both thought sleeping with someone was a valid enough explanation but the Meyers' laughter filled us with doubt.

Diane had chosen to ignore them both and had returned to her search. She walked slowly along the edge of the curb, touching the toe of her sneaker to every pebble or bit of debris. Between her fingers she rolled what had been thus far the morning's best find: the dark black earpiece to one of the hoods' sunglasses.

Mickey Meyer was saying, "It doesn't take more than five minutes. The guy gets on top of the girl"—he slammed his fist into his palm three times, imitating some adult—"and she's going to have a baby."

I thought of my parents and their breathless nights and early mornings. Of Leela's ruined marriage. "Maybe," I added.

"What do you mean *maybe*?" Mickey asked.

"Not always," I said. "It doesn't always work out."

From the curb where he sat, Ricky added, "Only if the guy sweats."

We all turned to him, even Mickey. This was a new part of the puzzle.

"What?" Georgie said, returning some of the Meyers' own scorn.

Ricky shrugged nonchalantly. "The guy's got to sweat, and the lady's got to drink it."

Diane, who was still pretending not to listen, was the first to say, "Does not," but we all quickly followed.

"Does," Ricky insisted.

"Who told you that?" I asked.

"My father," Ricky said.

"He did not!" Mickey cried.

"Yes he did," Ricky told him calmly.

"When?" Mickey demanded.

"Once," Ricky said, vague and arrogant with our attention. "When you weren't around."

Mickey squinted at him. "When wasn't I around?" He said it as if the very idea of his ever not being around was ludicrous.

"Last night," Ricky said regally. "When Dad got home from the police. You were sleeping. That's when he told me."

"Baloney!" Mickey cried.

Diane said, "That makes me sick just to think of it."

Ricky shrugged. "Glad I'm not the girl."

Georgie suddenly sat down beside him, chunky and puzzled, his round little mouth wide open and his brown shorts pulling against his white thighs. I recalled sometimes seeing light beads of sweat on his upper lip. "Is that what Sheryl did?" he asked.

"I guess," Ricky said.

"She did not," I told them impatiently. I knew the Meyers were notorious liars, but I also knew they usually collaborated on their tales. Their disagreement had given Ricky's story new authority. "It doesn't happen like that," I said.

"How, then, Miss Smarty?" Ricky asked.

I was about to say they kissed each other and breathed a baby into life but knew even before I spoke the words that it was a weak and fanciful explanation. I recalled my parents' voices, my mother's desperate headstand, Leela's tears and what Sheryl herself had told me. I knew something more difficult was involved.

Diane sighed loudly as if she hadn't wanted to reveal this but could no longer resist. "It had to do with where you go to the bathroom," she said quickly. "But you have to be married."

Now Georgie, his face lightening, changed his allegiance once more. Yes, he said. Diane was right. When his mother had her babies they tried to get out her behind, but the doctor cut open her stomach and took them out that way instead.

Mickey Meyer, still subdued by the possibility that their father had told Ricky something he hadn't told him, perked up a bit at this. "They cut open her stomach?" he cried. "Didn't all the food fall out?"

"Stupid," Diane whispered, and Ricky once more commanded center stage. "That's how they get out," he said. "But I'm talking about how they get in." He leaned forward and made each word emphatic. "The guy sweats and the lady drinks it, I swear."

"They do not," Diane said again, and Mickey suddenly leaned closer to her. He wore that look he got whenever he had something disgusting to show you: a blackened fingernail, a festering cut, a green opaque marble that he could hold in his nostril. "Maybe it's not sweat she drinks," he said, leering as effectively as a nine-year old can leer. "Maybe it has to do with where you go to the bathroom."

We all cried at this, suddenly moving around as if our revulsion were physical. Georgie stood and walked halfway up Sheryl's lawn. Diane and I stepped up the curb and then down again and then, to show our true indignation, crossed to the curb on the other side of the street. Georgie then skirted Ricky, who was crawling along the grass pretending to choke, and joined us. Mickey danced after him

(Diane and I shouting, "Get out of here," all the while he approached) and then Ricky followed.

Now Sheryl's house was before us and we held our small mementos in our hands or rested them on our bare knees. Siting on the curb, we began again, slowly and more seriously now, trying words the way a locksmith might go through a large set of keys. I said *womb* and *seed* and *conception*, and Diane contributed *kissing, petting* and *blood*. Ricky insisted on repeating *sweat*, and Mickey would not give up *bathroom*, although it had been Diane's contribution from the start. (I recalled my parents' hollow voices, the swish of tub water.) Georgie tried *bed* and *sleeping* a few times but then conceded them when I said *car* and *darkness*.

We stretched our legs, bare and summer-brown, out into the street before us. We touched each other at our elbows and shoulders as we tried words as we might try key after key. Across the street, the ragged lawn and the drawn shades had already become for us just one more desolate sign of that household's manlessness, and it was Mickey Meyer who first said, "I wonder if she'll have a boy."

We paused to think about this for a moment, realizing for the first time, I think, that whatever difficult and extravagant feat had to be performed, whatever painful acrobatics, whatever horror, we, the children, were after all the end, the desired result—the culmination of our poor parents' most difficult task, their very motive.

Georgie said a boy would be the right age to play with his youngest brother. Diane and I said we'd soon be old enough to baby-sit. Although we'd heard it a hundred times, the Meyer twins began to recount for us the elaborate story of their surprise birth, how in the first minute of life, according to their father, they had both spat in each eye of the doctor, who had failed to predict twins.

Slowly, we began to see what poor things our parents' lives would have been had we not, after their urging and acrobatics and pain, agreed to arrive, stumbling as we did upon the one consolation it seemed no one had yet offered Sheryl: a child as marvelous as any one of us would be born.

Part
Two

IT IS ONLY after a certain age, twenty-five or so, when the distance between the child you were and the adult you have become has grown great enough to breed wistfulness, that lovers feel the need to bring one another home. Or perhaps it is only a dare. We have by that time become aware of and even resigned to what part of our parents we will never shake—the receding hairline, the petulance, the inability to say and sincerely mean, "It's only money"—and maybe we bring home this stranger who has claimed love and fidelity simply as a test: Love me, love my parents; love what I come from and what I will, with no more choice or volition, become.

But teenagers know better. They choose parking lots and movie theaters and public playgrounds for their meetings. They do most of their courting in the historical void of a moving car. Fresh from the frustrations and humiliations of parental I-know-all-about-you-but-it-doesn't-make-any-difference love, they do all they can to preserve, unsullied, this newfound land, this blank slate of a girlfriend or boyfriend. They pretend, until history and memory once again bind them to their age, to be reborn at sixteen.

In the year Sheryl dated Rick, she went to his house only three or four times and only when he had forgotten something, a jacket or a bottle or a ten-dollar bill. He never asked her inside. Pulling up to the curb, opening his door and putting out his leg even before the car had fully stopped, he would mumble, "Be right back," and leave her, the engine still running, the radio going. She would sit still in the middle of the seat, or occasionally lean over to tap the gas pedal with her foot when the engine began to stall.

It would never occur to her that he should invite her in, introduce her to his sister and his father, and his mother if she was there. She would not have seen any point to it.

On a dull afternoon during the single winter they spent together, Rick stopped at his house for cigarette money or a stack of quarters to use in the pinball machines at the alley. It had been raining, that gray, unpoetic rain of mid-winter in a dreary suburb. The sky was a high and solid mass of featureless clouds, the rain steady but unenthusiastic: Sheryl could barely hear it on the roof of his car. There were small streams of water running along the ragged curbs, and the shingles on some of the houses were stained like blotters with dark waterlines. At school that morning, the yellow lights of the classrooms had shone dirtily into the rain and the parking lot and she'd been tempted to skip, the sight of them so exhausted and discouraged her. But she knew Rick would be inside waiting for her by her locker.

The sound of the engine reared and the car shook a little. Sheryl touched the wheel and stretched her left foot to the gas pedal. She saw a white plume of exhaust rise into the rearview mirror and watched it dissipate in the rain. Rick took longer than usual and she glanced toward his door. It was still partially open, as he

had left it. She hoped his father wasn't delaying him with his unending requests for another pillow or another station on the TV, a
glass of milk, answer the phone, and why can't he bring his books
home with him just once? Her own father, she thought, had been
kind and forgiving and funny—everything she did, it seemed to her
now, had pleased and amazed him. She tallied, as she had been
doing since his death, one life for another, who would have been
missed more, her father or Rick's. Rick's was even older, she knew.
He should have died so her father could have lived. No one would
have felt that bad.

She looked toward the house, considered touching the horn,
but instead reached again for the gas pedal. The exhaust cloud,
pale gray but lighter and brighter than the air and the sky, filled
the rear-view mirror once more and continued to grow, rolling
and smoking as she pumped the gas again and again, the engine
yelling, threatening, wanting to get away. She watched the rear-
view mirror: the street and the black trees and the houses behind
her were nearly obliterated by the exhaust. They reminded her of a
child's blotched pencil drawing, now erased and made new again.
Here, start over. Her father was alive and Rick's had died, and
since she hadn't met him yet, she didn't even know it.

She took her foot from the gas and sat back to watch the vapor
slowly rise and disappear, the colorless street once again growing
clear. Rick was at the front door, but he was turned away, talking
to someone. When he stepped out of the house, she could see that
he was angry. And then a woman stepped out behind him. She
was small—Sheryl had always imagined that Rick's mother would
be tall and powerful, thick and ungainly dead weight—and dark,
like Rick. She wore a raincoat that she held tightly closed at the
waist and she ran after him in short, merry little steps. Rick ignored her until he got to the car and then he pulled open the door

and said, "My mother wants to meet you," quick and sullen. He got in and slammed the door—for a second Sheryl thought he was going to pull away—and then leaned forward to turn off the engine. He slumped behind the wheel. Sheryl touched his leather jacket, spattered with rain. There was no time for her to move to the far side of the seat.

The woman bent down to the window and smiled in at them. "Hello," she called as if they were a great distance from her. "You're Sheryl."

Sheryl nodded and said hello. Rick stared at the windshield.

"Well, I'm Rick's mom," she said. She said it proudly, as if she'd just been awarded the title. Despite her illness, she looked younger than she was. Her straight brown hair was pulled off her face with a velvet hairband, but the ends of it fell over her cheeks as she leaned toward them. Her eyes, Rick's eyes, were dark and wide-spaced, obviously weak and yet somehow alluring. Only the deep vertical line between them, as dark as a scar, and the raw yellow patch of psoriasis on her forehead, as if to indicate the source of her troubles, reminded Sheryl of where she spent her weekdays.

She continued to grip her raincoat. Her pale throat was bare. "You'll have to forgive me for coming out like this," she said, her voice still calling. "But I just got home myself and I'm not resettled yet."

Sheryl nodded. She saw a purple flush spreading across Rick's cheek and jaw. She wanted him to start the engine.

"I'm back and forth, you know," his mother said.

Sheryl said, "Yeah." She thought of reaching for the keys herself.

"But getting better all the time," the woman said with a laugh. The rain was beginning to dampen her hair. "Or so they tell me."

She smiled. "Or so they want to believe." She suddenly looked up at the sky. "It's too bad about this rain," she said.

Sheryl nodded. "I hate it."

Rick's mother dropped her eyes to the girl, seemed to look into her face and her lap and then her face again. A tremor, as quick and delicate as a pulse, passed over her features, through her lips and her cheeks and across her eyelids, so quickly it seemed a drop of rain had simply moved like a shadow across her face.

"I hate it too," she said. "It makes me think we've lost the sun and don't even know it."

Rick shot forward then, as if he'd had all he could bear, and started the car. The cloud of exhaust rose like a sail behind them. "We're going," he said.

She stepped back from the door, still smiling, but didn't say another word.

When they stopped at the end of the block, Rick said, "Did she go in?"

Sheryl turned to look over her shoulder and his. She expected to see her there for some reason, if only because crazy people were supposed to be unreliable. Were supposed to stand out in the rain.

Through the thin white exhaust she saw only the empty sidewalk and the street. "Yeah," she said. "She's gone." She saw him raise his dark glasses and peer under them into the rearview mirror, his eyes startling in their resemblance to hers.

"She just asked me for money," he said when they had begun driving again.

Sheryl sank down beside him and put her cheek to his wet coat. "What for?"

She watched the leafless trees pass and then the tall lampposts along the boulevard. "She wants to get out of here," he said, and they both knew that he meant not merely out of our town or our state or the wet midwinter climate, but the world itself.

When Sheryl arrived in Ohio, her aunt and uncle were waiting for her at the airport, smiling reproachful but sympathetic smiles. Her aunt kissed her. Her uncle took her flight bag, which was nearly empty and marked with the name of another airline but which she had believed to be as requisite as a ticket and a seatbelt. "Well," her aunt and uncle said together, recognizing in one word the severity and complexity of her problem but saying also that they would make the best of it. "Well, well."

Outside, the sun had nearly set. Sheryl had to turn to look behind her to see the clear streak of scarlet at the horizon and, pressing down upon it like a hand, the dark blue sky. In it, the evening star seemed a tiny keyhole that gave promise of a wide, white-silver room. She did not wonder what Rick was doing at that very moment (he was pulling into the parking lot outside the supermarket where she had worked, tossing a cigarette from his window), if he gazed at the same star, but thought instead that the sun set in the west and so this road took them east. Faced her toward home. She watched the road signs carefully as they passed.

She had expected a farmhouse. Not because her uncle was a farmer, she knew he did something for GM, but because her mother had told her they lived on four acres. Sheryl had no clear idea of how large an acre was, but she associated them with farming and couldn't imagine any other reason for having four.

But instead they pulled into a long flat driveway that led to a new raised ranch, sparsely landscaped and lit like a car lot. Bright spots illuminated the driveway and the garage and hung from under the eaves all around the house: two shone on the huge front door. With them, and the flat treeless land that stretched unbroken for as far as she could see in the new darkness, Sheryl felt for the first time that she had been exiled, sent to an outpost, to the very edge of something she could only define as home.

Her uncle slammed the trunk of the car and the sound seemed final and remote in the summer air.

The front door opened before she and her aunt and uncle had reached it, and their daughter, Sheryl's cousin Pam, called a mellifluous "Hello." She was in her late twenties or early thirties, pretty and wide-bottomed, with a round, dimpled face that for a moment as she smiled in the spotlight seemed stark white. She embraced Sheryl lightly but kept an arm around her as she led her into the house.

Inside, the hallway had a high ceiling and ended in a pair of steps, one that went down to a family room, another that led up to the rest of the house. Its walls were lined with family photographs, a gallery of sorts, meant either to give a new visitor an immediate one-stop introduction to the entire family and its history or to remind the family members themselves, each time they passed through the door, of the complex weave of faces and lives that had been spun to produce them. Sheryl saw her parents in their wedding clothes, the familiar, old-fashioned studio portrait of her grandmother at twenty-five, newly arrived in America. And again her parents, sitting on a couch somewhere, holding her, a toddler, between them.

Pam was talking about her obstetrician. "He got me through three kids and one almost," she said. "He looks like Dr. Zorba, doesn't he, Mom? But he's as nice as he can be." She said he had agreed to squeeze Sheryl in tomorrow morning.

They went up the stairs and down a short hallway to the room, between the kitchen and the bathroom, where Sheryl was to stay.

The TV room they called it, although the TV had apparently been removed and replaced by a small set of cardboard drawers covered in pink satin. The fold-out couch had already been opened and made up, and someone had put a can of hairspray and a number of half-empty perfume bottles on a table near the bed.

Pam helped her unpack her clothes, pausing more than once to hold up a skirt or a pair of jeans and to squeal, "How do you get into these?" She herself wore a pale blue shirtwaist with a thin plaid belt, loafers and white bobby socks. Her hair was a perfect flip. "Believe me," she said "They won't fit much longer."

She asked if Sheryl sewed, and the girl shook her head. "I'll teach you," Pam said. "It's not worth buying maternity clothes when you can just run something up on the machine. It'll be fun."

She sat on the edge of the bed. She talked incessantly in a bright, warm voice. Her younger brother, she said, was away at camp for the summer, a counselor. The older one lived in St. Louis. Her own house was just a mile or two away. She'd bring her kids over in the morning. She couldn't wait for Sheryl to meet them. She said she knew three kids weren't that many, compared to some people, but it was enough to make her feel she could answer any questions Sheryl had. "For instance," she said, "I had a saddle block for the last one." She arched her back and reached behind her. "That's when they put a needle right into your spine. You don't feel anything from the waist down and it's marvelous. But you're awake enough to actually see the baby be born. I mean, if you want to."

Sheryl watched her from the other side of the room, her brush in her hand.

"Of course," Pam went on, "you can just be knocked out. That's not bad either."

Until this moment, Sheryl had not thought seriously about the baby to be born. Until now, she thought of the pregnancy itself as her dilemma, as if it were, in itself, a complete fact, without implication. All she had feared in the past two months was the moment she would have to walk into her mother's bedroom to tell her, and she had considered her punishment, the consequence of her confession, to be only the cold, humiliating examination she had had that morning, and then this exile.

Now she saw it was endless. It stretched infinitely before her, as fully burdensome as all the years she had yet to live.

"Father Tom at the church," Pam went on, adding to it, "will put you in touch with a wonderful agency, and you can be sure the family will be Catholic. He'll tell you all about it if you want. Whenever you're ready. He's a doll."

Sheryl turned to place her brush on the flimsy dresser.

"I'll make some calls about your school situation. You can probably do something like a correspondence course while you're here. You could get books from the high school here in September. I'm going to see if a friend of mine can come over and help you out. She taught before her kids came."

Sheryl heard her aunt in the kitchen, dropping ice cubes into glasses. She heard a sound, remote and faint, like the rumble of trucks on some distant highway. She would have to get up early to see where the sun rose.

"What would you like to have," Pam asked softly just as the aunt called, "Girls—iced tea!" "A boy or a girl?"

Sheryl paused for a moment. She had heard the word whispered among the neighborhood women from time to time, on those mornings when my own mother had returned from the hospital empty-handed, and had slowly come to understand its meaning. She had learned there was a sense of disappointment in it, but no threat or damage. It meant simply that a certain future had failed to arrive. That all had gone back to what it was, to what it had been before.

She tossed her hair defiantly and turned to face her cousin. "I'd like to have a miscarriage," she said.

Even as Pam flinched, her mouth closing with the shock of the word, Sheryl saw that she also forgave her. "You say that now," she said softly. "But just wait. You won't always feel that way."

"I will," Sheryl said, but she saw there would be no convincing her.

"Talk to me in six more months," Pam said. "You'll see."

That evening, with her aunt and uncle safely in bed, Sheryl walked down the stairs to the hallway with the photographs and then down the second set of steps to the family room. She placed a pillow over the phone there, dialed the number she had written in ink on the inside of her arm, the same number she had dialed from the airport when she had told her mother she was going to the bathroom. Then it had rung and rung, but now it was snatched up before the first ring had barely begun, as if someone had been waiting for it. Not Rick, though; it was a woman's voice that said hello. Sheryl asked for him in a whisper.

The only light in the room came from the bright spot outside and made the linoleum floor seem black, threw bars of light and shadow across the couch where she sat. There was too long a pause before the voice said another hello. Sheryl realized that this woman, too, was whispering.

"May I speak to Rick?" she said again, raising her voice a bit.

The woman, his mother, raised hers a bit as well. "He's not here," she said. "He's gone out." There was another pause, filled only with the hollow sound of the line, the distance between them. Sheryl imagined the woman in a darkened room like this one, cupping the receiver to her lips.

"This is Sheryl," she said, and the woman softly repeated her name, exclaiming it in a throaty whisper. And then, as if they were exchanging secrets, "This is Rick's mom."

"Will you tell him I called?" Sheryl said. The woman was silent, and Sheryl rushed on, "Will you tell him I'm at my aunt's house," the receiver so close to her mouth she wondered briefly if it might have been stopping her words rather than carrying them, "in Ohio." She paused and listened for her aunt or uncle's footsteps. On the other end, beyond the static, she could sense Rick's mother listening to the house behind her, too, touching her fingertips to the dry patch on her head.

"Will you tell him?" she said again, although she knew even then that she would not. "Will you please tell him?" It struck her as familiar, this repetition of what she knew already was a futile, a meaningless, plea.

"I don't know where he is," Rick's mother whispered. "I'm back and forth, you know."

"I know," Sheryl said. "But tell him, will you? I don't know when I can call again."

"Sure," the woman murmured, seeming to address someone else in the room, although Sheryl was quite certain there was no one else there, that Rick's mother had been wandering like a ghost through her own darkened house when the phone rang; that she was as much a frightened stranger in it as Sheryl was in this one.

When the woman hung up, abruptly and without another word, Sheryl slipped quietly up the stairs and into her room, stopping for just a moment at the closet in the hallway to search the pockets of the coats hanging there for spare change, as Rick had told her his mother used to do whenever she was preparing to leave them.

———

The four acres, Sheryl learned, were not all barren, nor did they stretch evenly all around. She saw with the light that there were other houses on either side of her aunt and uncle's and, at the far end of their property, a line of trees that marked the edge of a highway. She was not certain if it was the highway on which she had come, but it was a highway nonetheless and given enough time she could walk to it.

Pam drove her downtown to the doctor's office the next morning, where the old man smiled at her with wet pale blue eyes. When he had finished his exam, he grasped her forearm and shook it a little, then patted her shoulder (the one gesture meaning bear up; the other, soon it will be over), just as so many people had done the day of her father's funeral.

As they were leaving, he took her chin in his hand and ran a flat thumb over a spattering of pimples there. "Why do you want to hide such a pretty face behind so much makeup?" he asked her.

She lowered her eyes, her cheeks burning. What she had done with Rick, what had brought her here, had been done in darkness and without words and had made her feel completely adult. These men in their bright offices seemed bent on reversing that. As if humiliation, a confirmation of her immaturity, were part of her treatment and cure. Or as if their smiling ministrations would win her back her childhood.

When they left the office, Pam asked if she'd like to look at some patterns.

Sheryl said, "I really don't care," and then followed her into a large old variety store where the floors were wood and almost soft with wear and the air smelled of plastic and popcorn. Sheryl went to the makeup counter first. Her mother had given her a twenty-dollar bill when she got on the plane, promising to send more later. Sheryl's father used to say that money burned a hole in her pocket, but when she handed the bill to the cashier (she bought lipstick and turquoise-blue eyeshadow, another mascara and a thick blue compact, daring her cousin to repeat the doctor's words), she felt a real sense of loss, almost a fear, and she quickly folded the change, the broken bill, into her palm.

In the notions department, Pam led her to three pattern books as big as dictionaries, with thick, glossy pages. She flipped them over expertly, found the right section and then turned the pages for Sheryl as if she were a child.

"Just stop me when you see something you like," she said, but then paused at every other page herself to coo over the pastel drawings of pregnant women in loose blouses and skirts, dresses as wide and roomy as tents, all with bows and ruffles and appliqués, all somehow infantile.

"This would look cute on you," Pam would say. Or, "Oh, I like this one."

Sheryl stood at her side, watching silently. At the end of the section (Sheryl noticed that formals were next, prom gowns and bridesmaid dresses, as if the pattern people had gotten their chronology as backward as she had), Pam turned to her. "Anything?" she asked brightly.

Again she merely shrugged. Pam went to the next book and repeated the process, but silently this time. As she moved on to the third, she said, her eyes on the pages and her voice low for what seemed the first time, "You know, Sheryl, I'd really like to be your friend." She paused and there was only the sound of the store: a cash register ringing and someone calling, "Miss, Miss." "I know you're having a hard time right now. And I know you think you don't need anybody else, but let me tell you, you do." She laughed, almost bitterly. "Believe me, even under the best of circumstances you need a friend, a girlfriend, to help you through what you're about to go through. You really do." She turned to look at her. Her small eyes were green and there was a dimple in her round fleshy chin. She had a fine yellow moustache. "I'm trying to be your friend."

Sheryl stepped back a little, aware already of all that had begun to insinuate itself between them: her cousin and her uncle and her aunt, their big house, this town, the baby to be born, even the hours since she'd last seen him—all coming between them when she'd promised it couldn't happen.

She spoke sullenly. "I know it," she said. "You don't have to tell me, I know it."

She felt Pam watching her for a moment and then heard her sigh, impatiently, and continue turning pages. Suddenly and almost against her will, Sheryl raised her hand. She saw her own round finger on one of the glossy pages. She had not been spoken to so directly, had not had anyone but Rick so directly meet her eye, since her father had died.

"I like this one," she said quickly.

THAT NIGHT THEY GATHERED EARLY, in the middle of a deserted dead-end street by the reservoir. This was the starting point for drag races, the scene of a much talked about rumble between another set of car-driving hoods and a motorcycle gang from the next town, the place where many of them, Rick included, had once crashed through the high weeds and fallen flat on their stomachs, walkie-talkies and toy machine guns in their hands. (And one of them always stepped in dog dirt; one of them always found something odd and evil: an old rubber glove, a toilet seat, a damp and muddy magazine.) It was a no-man's-land, a blank space in the neighborhood. A street with a broken curb but no sidewalks, no driveways, no homes. Just tangled grass and trees and tall yellow weeds and a high chain-link fence beyond which the earth seemed to end, dipping as it did into the steep-sided and dried-out reservoir. Years and years ago, a child had drowned there and so all the following generations of children—including my own—were told it was off bounds. It still retained that sense of the forbidden.

By now they had a plan. First, Rick wouldn't take his own car. The old lady would recognize it in a minute and maybe call the cops. He'd ride in the back seat of the middle car. They'd cruise by a couple of times just to check the place out, make sure they were home. They'd drive real slow, just kind of loop around. If somebody called the police, no problem. "'Hey, officer.'" Rick held out his hands innocently. His dark glasses reflected the pale blue sky, the faces of the others as they leaned over the opened doors of their cars. "'We're just practicing our driving skills, that's all. We're just killing time until the nine o'clock movie, that's all.' What are they going to do, say you can't drive on this street—'Which street? We've been on every one of them.'"

The other boys nodded, or simply stirred in agreement, as the fathers would later do.

"And when do we make our move?" one asked.

Rick turned his head slowly, looking at them all. "Let's just see," he said. "Let's just get over there and check it out."

They slapped the roofs of their cars. "Right," they said. "C'mon." "Let's go."

Rick slipped into the back seat of the middle car. Two boys slipped in on either side of him. Already he was staring straight ahead, like someone trying to outpsyche a roller coaster. The two boys glanced at him and then at one another. One of them touched the chains piled on the floor with the toe of his black boot.

"We're out of here," the driver said.

They followed the side streets toward Sheryl's house, looping around them, doubling back. The streets near the reservoir were a bit less prosperous; there were smaller, prewar houses with high windows and doors, narrow alleyways between them. There were gnomes and bird baths in many of the front yards, or statues of Mary or Saint Francis tucked into egg-shaped grottoes painted sky blue within and covered without by sea shells pressed into the cement. There were clotheslines, like the skeletons of umbrellas, stuck into every side yard.

It was still dinnertime and so there were few people on the street. Whiffs of garlic and grilled meat came across the summer air. A young woman wearing a plaid bathing suit sat in a lawn chair on her narrow driveway, a baby with a saggy diaper standing before her. She looked up as they passed. They circled her block and went by her again.

They headed east, away from the sun, which was still fairly high. Past a man in a brown business suit who was closing the gate that crossed his driveway, his car humming behind him. Past three children riding tricycles along the sidewalk, who only slowed their pace as the cars passed, in an odd counterpoint.

South now, through the oldest part of town, passing within two blocks, and then one, of Rick's father's old office. And then back again, briefly paralleling the boulevard. Inside, they were uncomfortable without their radios on, with the windows only partway down.

Now the neat and shaded streets. More dinnertime smells. They passed a grandmother standing out on a lawn, watering a flower bed filled with bright impatiens. She watched them over her shoulder. "Yeah, you too," one of the boys whispered.

At the next corner, they turned onto our block. As they approached her house, only Rick, pushed back between them, turned his head. The front door was wide open; the window fan was moving. There was no sign of her.

They paused at the stop sign, moved around the corner, one, two, three.

"Nothing," one of the guys said.

Rick said, "It's all right. Keep going." He folded his arms across his chest, his leather jacket creaking a little, popping as it pulled away from the shoulders of the other two boys. The car smelled of musk.

They continued on, around two blocks, turning off onto another. There was an ashtray built into the back of the front seat, and one of the boys suddenly leaned forward and popped it open, then pushed it closed. Rick looked at him, his mouth drawn.

"Just checking for scumbags," the boy said.

Rick gave a half smile.

"Left?" the driver asked.

"Yeah," Rick said. He watched him make the turn. "You ever get laid in this back seat, Victor?" His voice was low.

The driver glanced in the mirror. "Yeah," he said. "Every night."

"By what?" the boy beside him asked. "Your dog?"

"By your mother," Victor said.

"Victor gets laid," Rick told them generously. "He gets laid by all kinds of girls. He gets laid almost as much as I do."

They all chuckled, a little embarrassed, sensing he was hardening his heart.

Victor looked in his mirror again. "Nobody gets laid as much as you do, Rick."

It was no less a consciously kind statement because it was, or had been, true.

They turned onto her street again and made a left this time. A bald man stepping out of his car paused to look at them. Further down, a woman holding a white cake box and filling her back seat with little boys did the same. They passed the grandmother again who was now talking across a hedge to her neighbor, the green garden hose curled neatly against the side of her garage. They passed Angle's house. Its wrought-iron railing and front door and drainpipes were painted pale pink. Her father was out mowing the lawn.

They made a group of kids playing baseball in the street step out of their way. The kids moved only as far as they had to. They looked into the cars like curious, defiant natives, knowing that they would soon be teenagers too, that they would replace them.

They continued on, repeated another circuit and then headed back the way they had come, doubled back, added a few new streets to their route. They no longer missed the sounds of their radios. There was the hard, ripping drone of their engines. They could feel it in their feet and all up and down their legs.

The next time they passed her house, the boy in the front passenger seat of the first car gave the gathered audience his enormous Sergeant Bilko grin.

Rick sat low in his seat, staring out past the shoulders of his friends, through the green-tinted windshield that his own dark glasses made black. He was only vaguely aware of the passing shadows of trees, lights coming on here and there. He no longer thought of all the other days and nights he had passed by these houses and along these streets. None of it was familiar to him now. He saw it only from the corners of his eyes and what he saw seemed vague and indifferent, and somehow threatening in that indifference. Nothing else seemed to know that the world had changed in the past few days. Or not even changed, he thought, but become again, with a vengeance, what it had been before he met her: flat, uncaring, withdrawing all that it offered every time he put out his hand. Handing him jokes. He remembered a movie he had seen once as a kid, a scene from it that had bored itself into his nightmares: a little girl holding a bundle, a baby in a bonnet, squirming and crying. She tries to quiet it, begins singing a light song. The crying grows louder and louder and the squirming more violent. You wonder how a little baby can squirm so much. You're afraid she'll drop it. Then there's a nose, a little hoof flinging itself from the blankets. The girl looks down and sees it's not a baby at all but a pig—the baby has turned into a pig, or it had been a pig all along. She drops it with a start. The creature runs off, the satin bonnet flapping against its hide.

Everything he was handed withdrawn or suddenly, inexplicably, transformed. Waking from a nap, coming home from school or in from play to find that nothing in the flat, indifferent world had changed: the television might still be on, wet clothes might still be in the washer, a piece of meat left on the counter to thaw: only she had disappeared.

He could feel the sweat on his neck, smell the musky odor of the car and, mingling with it, the odor of cut grass. He could feel the heat of his friends pressed beside him.

"Right?" Victor said, and he nodded. The world swinging slowly across the dark windshield: house, lawn, lamppost, street. He would simply walk up to her front door.

"How much longer?" one of them asked.

"Give it time," he said. The streetlights were touching the cars, the back windshield of the car in front, the hood and doors of the one he rode in, the one behind, rolling over them again and again. His friends shifted their feet; the chains on the floor made a small clink.

"Not too late," one of them was saying. "You don't want it to be too dark."

"No," Rick told them. "I know when."

He would simply walk up to her front door. He'd done it a million times already. He would make everything be the same, push back the time, wrestle whatever had changed to the floor. He didn't care if it took a million friends, a hundred cars, chains the size of boulders. He would make it go back to what it was. She had said it herself, she had promised him: nothing else would matter to them, friends, family, getting older, good luck or bad.

The lights were passing slowly over the cars. The engines were straining to keep their slow and steady pace. They moved invisibly now, no one watching, no one coming to their windows or their doors.

He would simply go into her house and pull from it what had been. He would say no for the first time. He would say, No, I'm not taking it, I'm not taking this. His mother disappearing, standing right before him and disappearing, taking with her that part of him she had filched when she was well. His father drawing in, curling into a ball, his skin, hair, bones, voice growing thinner and thinner by the hour, his father getting ready to disappear.

As a kid, he had imagined forcing open her mouth, reaching his hand in, pulling his real mother out the way the hunter had pulled the swallowed citizens from the wolf's stomach. He had imagined, just yesterday, just this morning, kicking the crutches out from under his father's arms, bending his back straight, forcing him to return.

It was the same: He would walk calmly up to her front door. He had his friends, the wide engines of these three heavy cars, the chains. He would make it go back to what it was.

They turned slowly, one, two, three, onto Sheryl's block. Victor gripped the wheel.

"You know what to do," Rick said, encouraging him.

Victor nodded. "We know."

He pressed himself into the seat, between the fat leather shoulders of his friends. He would simply walk up to her front door: nothing's changed. The other boys were tense and silent. Their scent suddenly moved like a draft through the car.

The sound was violent, blinding. The first car gunned and spun and Victor's arms were moving in wide, quick arcs over the steering wheel. They felt the leap, the banging over the curb, the sound. The sound of it seemed unbelievable. And then the doors on one side swung open. Everything outside was still.

He knew he had done it as soon as his boot touched the walk. The exhaust hung in the air like gunpowder, like magician's dust. He had done it. Wasn't the house there as it always had been before? Wasn't he walking toward it as he had done a million times before, the sound of his heels neat and confident?

He calmly mounted the steps, politely rattled the front door. He slipped his hands into his back pockets, waiting. Then he leaned forward, cupping his hands to his eyes. There was the familiar living room, dimmed by the screen, drained of color. In a minute, he would enter it, as he'd done so many times before. In a minute, she would come, smiling to see him.

Something moved in the shadows. He stepped away. Hadn't he done it? Wasn't he back?

That night Sheryl and Pam laid out the pattern they had bought on the living room floor. Pam showed Sheryl how to use the dart wheel and tracing paper, how to cut in a straight line with pinking shears, to match fabrics and baste seams. She set up the ironing board and ironed the material with every step, the smell of old starch and steam filling the warm air. Pam's husband and children were down in the family room with her parents, watching television, but Roger, the youngest, kept wandering up to see what his mother and Sheryl were doing. Eventually, he stayed. He stretched out on the floor beside them as they cut the material, and then fell asleep while Sheryl guided the material through the machine, Pam standing over her. He slept like an infant, his cheek flat against the carpet and his mouth open, his arms straight at his side, the back of his small hands to the floor. When the dress was finished but for the hem and buttons, Pam went into the kitchen to make popcorn and pour Cokes for everyone. Idly, Sheryl knelt beside the sleeping child, running her hand back and forth through the thick carpet.

At about ten o'clock, Pam and her husband got ready to go home. Her husband was tall and blond, not handsome but somewhat sweet and comical in his Bermuda shorts. Sheryl watched him as he gently lifted Roger from the floor. The child whimpered a little as he rose through the air, but then settled against his father's body as if it had been made for his rest, the shoulder carved to fit his cheek, the arm bent simply to cradle him.

This evening, each time she had gone into her room to try on the new dress, Sheryl had noticed the swelling in her stomach and breasts. Lulled for the moment by the calm industry of the evening, by the pleasant house filled with more family than she had ever known, she had thought with some curiosity and a kind of pride of the baby she carried, the child she would be mother to. She had even stood sideways before the mirror, her hands on her stomach, her eyes meeting her own in the mirror, large and soulful, the classic pregnant madonna pose. She had even smiled.

But now as she watched her cousin's husband turning casually and only a little stiffly to see where the other two children had gone, the little boy asleep against him, she felt only a dazzling and depthless loss. Not because her own child would never know its father, the father never know what rest his body had been formed to give, but because she was not the child she had once been but would never be again. Because the shoulder and chest and arms that had once so casually and so thoroughly held her had left the earth long before she had lost her need for them.

She cried out, a short, breathless shout, or, in the bustle of their departure, merely stood silently, tears in her eyes.

Seeing her, hearing her, Pam turned and said, "Oh, honey," as if something precise and delicate had toppled over, so close to its completion.

Sheryl turned from them all and went into her room alone.

At eleven-thirty, her mother called to say, in a thin and angry voice that made her seem a stranger, "Well, we had a visit from your boyfriend tonight."

Sometime later, when most of the lights had been extinguished around the house and Sheryl lay awake in her strange bed, Pam came into her room. She was back from her own house, where she had gotten her children to sleep, and then returned just to speak to her. (For in her fierce sympathy, her boundless energy, she had made Sheryl her project, her quest, had taken her on as a few years later she might take on a career, a degree, a lover, a few years later when the chasm that was now at the heart of her life as a mother and a wife had been revealed to her as something shared and justifiable and capable of being healed only by a virtuous selfishness.)

Seeing Sheryl was awake, or hearing her crying from the hallway, she stepped into the dark room. From the window came a pale blue light, the outer edge of the one light that was kept on throughout the night. It fell through the corner of the shade in a straight bar. She stood by the girl's bed, a reverse silhouette, pale against the darkness but without detail.

Whispering, she asked if she could stay, if she could speak. Sheryl only turned toward her, her eyes alone catching the bit of light and shining briefly with it.

The squeak of the thin bedframe, the heavy weight on the mattress and the rustle of Sheryl's legs beneath the sheet as she

moved them away. The house was quiet but for the distant rumble
of a passing truck. The air was hot and humid.

"Honey," she began. She began with a gentle attempt to con-
vince the girl that she understood perfectly what she was feeling.

"I know how hard this is for you." "I know this is a difficult
time." "I know this isn't easy."

And then, to win her to her side, "I know how much you must
have loved your boyfriend."

The blue light lying like a bandage along the side of her face,
along the fleshy shoulder and bare arm. "You probably miss him a
lot. Your mom said you saw him every day. It must be terrible, suddenly being separated like this. I remember."

The story she then told was as all attempts at sympathy are: an
effort to match in form and size and detail what another has
known: to hold one experience next to another the way lovers and
children match fingers and hands, as if these two, side by side, are
linked by their likeness, are both identical and unique.

"I was once in love with a boy, too. When I was just about your
age. And we were separated. And I thought I would never be able
to go on living. I thought I'd kill myself or die of a broken heart—
just not wake up some morning after crying all night." There was a
facetiousness in her voice that Sheryl could not fail to hear. The
smirk behind the words of an adult who has too readily joined a
child's game. Her cousin was old enough, had been married long
enough, to know that this sort of love was not it, this romantic love
for a boyfriend or young husband was not, after all, what lasted;
that it was foolish, even adolescent to believe it might. She was
young enough in her life as a mother to feel quite certain that only
the love she had for her children was worth the drama and intensity
the young gave to one another. It was what she had meant when she

told Sheryl, just wait: it was the only love that could even begin to match the other's foolish claims.

"But every morning I did get up," she went on. "I didn't die. And days kept on, one after the other, and things slowly began to change. I began to feel better, little by little. Little by little, I thought of other things. I met someone else. I got over it."

In the dark room, in the single shaft of the blue nightlight—the light kept burning merely to demonstrate to the night that the family in this house is watchful, determined to be safe—it is the only wisdom an adult can offer the child. It is both an incantation and a prayer: You will and you must. Not merely get over the loss, but also learn that its insult is not nearly as great as it once seemed.

"I know it doesn't seem possible now, but in a few years you'll be different and what seems like a terrible loss to you now will only seem natural, a small part of your life. You'll have trouble remembering just how you feel today and why. You'll meet someone else. You'll have other children, lots of them, and then you'll see. You'll be happy."

What she couldn't have known, in her sympathy, her easy wisdom (for she was right, it would happen even to Sheryl exactly as she had said), was how the girl had linked her father and Rick, the way she had determined to love them. She couldn't have known that for Sheryl, bereft as she was, peace was annihilation and to say that love could fade, that loss could heal, was to admit forever that there would be no return of the dead.

THAT NIGHT SHERYL GOT OUT of bed while the pale blue light still shone through her window. She dressed in a tight pair of black jeans and a loose yellow shell that was stretched out enough to cover her open fly and the thick rubber band she now used to fasten her waist. She put on her makeup in the dark, brushed and teased her hair, then filled her pocketbook with her comb and her makeup, a can of deodorant and one of the half-empty bottles of perfume. She left her room with her shoes in her hand. In the living room, the windows glowed with a vague light, but the center of the house, the hallway before her, the carpet beneath her feet, was dark and indefinite. She could hear the distinct, inharmonious sounds of her aunt's and uncle's breathing, one sighing long sighs that seemed to end each time with a click or a kiss, one sawing hollow logs, angry and insistent.

She went again to the hall closet, carefully slid open the door and reached inside. She moved one hand down the length of each coat sleeve and into each pocket, hoping each time to be surprised by the feel of a coin. She found a dime in her aunt's raincoat, a quarter and a nickel in her uncle's slick windbreaker. She now had nearly twelve dollars. This evening when her mother had called, shrill and tearful with the tale of Rick's visit, Sheryl had asked her to send more money. She dismissed the request impatiently. "What do you need money for?" she'd snapped. "Haven't you got everything you need?"

Sheryl couldn't say, "I need it to get out of here."

There was a small high window in the front door, and as Sheryl turned from the closet, she saw that the pale light that came through it caught some of the picture frames on the opposite wall and made the glass shine blankly, as if the faces and figures beneath had somehow vanished. But she knew which one she wanted simply by its shape, and she lifted it carefully and slipped it into her bag. She turned quickly and descended the next set of steps. She crossed the family room, the linoleum cold against her bare feet, and quickly opened the door. She had already begun to perspire, but the air was cool and she felt a wave of nausea as she hit the grass. She began to walk toward the spot where she knew the sun would rise.

It was still dark, but what stars there had been were nearly gone and the air seemed close. She held out her hand as she walked, occasionally brushing at her cheeks and her bare arm as if she felt someone's breath upon them. The ground, which had looked flat and fairly even from the house, was riddled with sockets and hills and small weeds that scratched at her bare ankles. She stumbled once or twice and began to feel frightened. But then her eyes grew accustomed to the darkness and soon she could make out a distant line of trees.

When she had gone a good distance from the house she put her pocketbook down, slipped the rubber band from the button at her waist and squatted. She could see the spotlight on the side of the house, white and sharp as a low star. She tried to make herself believe she would never return to this place, that it would be forever a small and ever fading part of her past, but her time there had been too short, her memory even now too new and indistinct. It seemed more a future she had only, briefly, glimpsed than a part of her history, left behind her. When she stood again, she saw how round and white her belly was in the darkness.

There was a heavy underbrush beneath the trees and she could hear birds waking as she passed. She put her pocketbook on her head to keep the bats out of her teased hair and raised her legs high with each step as if she were walking through snow. She caught her foot in a vine and, stumbling, swung her pocketbook into the trunk of a tree. There was the sound of metal and glass. A dog barked somewhere in the distance.

There was a high fence at the edge of the trees and she climbed it quickly, the metal singing, the wires familiar in her fingers—the heady swing over the top. Then down a steep hill, which she took at a run, and she was at the edge of the highway. It was deserted and, except for her own heavy breathing, silent. Just across it, the sky was turning a weak orange, but the wide road itself was still deep gray. The grass that split it and continued on the other side was still as dark as the sky behind her. There was a high white light off to her right and a single star at the horizon. She stood for a minute trying to catch her breath, to figure out what side of the road she should stand on. She had imagined it would run east and west; north and south was no good to her.

She backed up a little and lowered herself onto the grass. Her hand was trembling when she lit a cigarette, and when she wiped her wrist across her forehead it glistened with sweat. Her shoes were damp, and she rubbed a line of mosquito bites along her ankle.

In the darkness and the silence, she tried to think of Rick but knew he would be asleep now, unconscious; his anger or his fear or whatever it was that he'd felt as he pulled her mother from the house would be as good as forgotten at this moment. She recalled a night last winter when they'd both fallen asleep in his car and had woken cold and startled, lost in the world and momentarily strangers. If he were woken now, at this minute, if she called him on the phone at this minute, he couldn't say where she was or even that he thought of her. No one could.

She heard a car approaching on the opposite side and for a second believed it was Pam, out looking for her, already determined to retrieve her. But the car passed quickly with a flash of headlights and Sheryl could see nothing beyond its black windows.

There was a kind of loneliness in its wake, a tense new edge to the silence.

In the minute before he died, her father had pulled his car to the side of the road, loosened his tie and raised one leg to the seat beside him. He must have thought of her and of her mother, but they hadn't known it. She was drawing elaborate butterflies in the margins of her algebra exam. Her mother was on the phone with Mrs. Sayles when the policeman came to the door.

Sheryl tossed the cigarette into the road and rested her chin on her hands. His bracelet gleamed in the half light, but when she put her cheek to it, it seemed ice-cold. She sat back suddenly to ease the strain of fabric against her waist. She searched the horizon for that one star, but it had already faded in the growing light.

Had they been more vigilant in their love, she was certain, they would have saved him. The car in the driveway would have signified his return.

Another car approached, on her side this time, and she stood quickly and held her thumb out. It sped by her, the grit and the hot air stinging her eyes. Again she hadn't been able to see anyone inside, and the ensuing silence made her feel she was dreaming. She had an urge to shout, to test her voice. She felt a rising panic in her throat.

Three more cars passed, ignoring her, but the fourth stopped a good way down the road and then backed up as she ran toward it. She saw the driver through a haze of stinging tears. He was young, with a dark crew cut. He had to lower the radio to ask her, "Where you headed?"

"East," she said.

He leaned across the seat to open the door. Their sudden speed struck her as miraculous.

By the time the sun began to set, she had almost completely lost her bearings, and although her last ride, two teenage girls about her own age, had assured her that the exit where they had left her led to a road that traveled due east, she hesitated trying it. By now she was certain her aunt and her mother had the police out looking for her and she would have to find some back roads to make her way on. She'd had nothing to eat all day but the few potato chips the girls had shared with her and a bottle of Coke a trucker had bought her in West Virginia.

She turned back to the road the girls had taken, a smaller tar road that seemed to have risen in the middle like a loaf of bread. She walked along a dry gully at its edge, the afternoon heat still burning through the soles of her shoes and making everything ahead seem to shimmer. Thick trees lined the road beside her and through them came an occasional yellow and blinding glare of the setting sun. It was the time of day and of summer that made her think of barbecues and sunburn. Going upstairs to dress for the hot summer night ahead. Dotting perfume behind her thighs.

She walked slowly, the pocketbook heavy in her hand. The cars that passed her seemed dangerously close; some tooted their horns as they went by her, but she tried not to veer. She felt a blister forming on her heel. The time of day and summer when she would lean across the tiny child's desk she had transformed into a vanity table with sheer white curtains, lean into the plastic mirror lined with round bulbs, the movie-star mirror she had gotten for her thirteenth birthday (her father looking truly puzzled when she opened it, looking across the dining room table, across the remnants of cake and ice cream to ask, "No more dolls?"), and draw perfect black lines across her eyelids.

She walked steadily through the dust and the heat, uncertain of where she was going but knowing that sooner or later she would come upon something. A place to rest and to eat. It had to be. There was the smell of hot tar in the air, the lingering odor of passing cars. The sun shot through the trees, red now, lower than it had been but still bright enough to make her squint. The time of day neighbors came out to their porches and their driveways, patting their bellies and sucking their teeth. When she would wait to hear Rick's boots on the steps, the thrilling rattle at the door.

The darkness had begun to come in like water, filling up the wells already formed by the shadows of trees and leaves, when she saw a white sign at the edge of the road ahead and then came upon a small restaurant, squat and low with brown shake shingles and a wide, dusty lot.

There was a cigarette machine in the entry and a long, green-topped counter across the far wall, red plastic booths and stools. The waitress who leaned against one looked up as she came in. Just over her shoulder, there was a narrow pass-through window from the kitchen. The cook behind it looked at her, too, only a nose and a pair of eyes.

Sheryl walked quickly to the furthest corner and slid into a booth, refusing to meet anyone's gaze. She lit a cigarette and immediately turned to the window.

The waitress was about her mother's age, short and plump, and she said, "Isn't it hot?" as she swabbed the table with a gray rag. She wore a charm bracelet and a thin wedding band. Her arm was freckled.

Sheryl said, "Yes, it is."

"Is there just going to be you?" the woman asked.

Sheryl paused for a moment, uncertain.

"Are you waiting for someone?" the waitress said.

Sheryl shook her head. "Oh," she said. "No." And she began the lie she had rehearsed: "My mother dropped me off."

But the waitress merely nodded and set one napkin before her. "You want a Coke?"

Sheryl said yes. When the waitress brought it, she ordered a hamburger and french fries and then asked, "Is it all right if I use the bathroom?"

The woman laughed. She had a small flat nose and narrow eyes. "Sure. I won't let anybody sit here."

In the bathroom, Sheryl dug out her makeup and saw the glass over the picture had cracked in two places. She ran her index finger over one of the cracks and was surprised to see blood streak the glass. She looked at her finger and only slowly felt the pain. She put the picture on the sink and ran cold water over the cut. In the photograph, her mother and father were young-looking and smiling, her father with his mouth open a little, as if he were saying something. She, a toddler, was sitting between them. There was something old-fashioned about their clothes, her mother's plaid skirt and her father's white socks and black shoes. Something old about the chalky colors of the picture.

Months after her father died, her mother had said suddenly at dinner one summer evening, "I can't remember what Daddy sounded like." She seemed about to panic, as if she had just lost the memory and knew it could not be retrieved. "I can't think of how he sounded, can you?"

Sheryl had said of course she could. She would remember it always. But what she really remembered, she knew, were the words he had used, "Holy cow," and "Let's everybody keep a level head." The sound she gave him was the sound of her own voice, repeating the words he had used or merely imagining others. His real voice and the words he had actually used, what he'd been saying the second the photograph was taken, for instance, was lost to her, although she hadn't realized it until her mother asked if she could still remember.

She returned the picture to her pocketbook and slowly reapplied her makeup, studying her eyes and her lips and her round flat face to see what the people she had ridden with today had seen, what the waitress and the cook saw. If, adrift as she was, she had changed. She lifted her arms and sprayed herself with deodorant. Combed her bangs and reteased her hair. Her shell rode up over her belly and as she pulled it down she saw the imprint of her open fly. She lifted the blouse, tucking the hem of it under her chin, and tried once more to pull up her zipper, to close the button at her waist. But even though she held her breath, the rubber band merely buckled a little, her belly only strained against it. She pulled her blouse over her waist again and saw clearly that she hadn't fooled anyone.

She left the bathroom carrying her pocketbook before her like a child.

Back at the table, she ate slowly, feeling the others watching her. Each time the cook finished an order, he glanced through his window toward her. An elderly woman in the next booth smiled at her each time she looked up from her plate. The men at the counter turned indifferently to glance at her over their shoulders. There were some teenagers at a table in the opposite corner, two teenage couples and an extra boy. The girls giggled continuously while the boys grew louder and louder in their talk. Sheryl gathered they were all going to a movie nearby. She knew the single boy had somehow lost his date.

She ordered coffee simply to seem older and then apple pie, although she would have preferred chocolate cake, for the same reason.

"Your mom going to pick you up?" the waitress asked.

Sheryl shook her head. "No. I'm supposed to meet her down the road. At the gas station. Our car broke down and she had to take it there to get it fixed."

The waitress frowned a little, and Sheryl added, as she had rehearsed, "She doesn't know anything about cars. She's a widow."

The woman threw back her head. "Tell her to learn," she said. "I'm a widow, too, and not three weeks after my husband died some mechanic took me for a hundred dollars. Tell your mom to take an adult ed course or something. Where you from?"

"Ohio," Sheryl said. "Columbus."

"Tell your mom to see if they have a course at your high school. I know. It's tough when you're alone."

Two more teenagers came in and the waitress went to them. When Sheryl stood to leave, she felt the eyes of the faceless cook follow her to the register. The waitress took her money and gave her her change.

"'Night now," she said, looking at her carefully.

Sheryl said, "Good night."

A small decal on the door said the place closed at ten.

She returned to the road, continued walking. She had thought she might simply walk all night, but the blister on her heel was sharply painful—she paused to wedge a tissue between it and the back of her shoe, but it didn't help—and the road was so black she occasionally missed her step, thinking the earth rose where it did not or failing to see where it fell. There was a thin moon skimming the trees, gray and marbled like a worn shell. She turned and walked back to the diner.

Behind the parking lot were the remains of a rotting stockade fence. It was surrounded by high grass, and as soon as she made her way around it, she could hear the shrill drone of a mosquito in her ear, but there was a safety in it. She sank down in the grass, her back to the damp wood. The stars above the trees looked pale green. The moon rose higher. She listened to the cars coming and going over the dirt, the footsteps and the voices, simply waiting. She never thought that tomorrow she would be back home, with Rick, all returned to what it had been. She settled instead for a smaller return, to a place where she had rested and had something to eat. She would simply be grateful to see the sun once more, the night over. A day like the last beginning again.

There was a good half hour of silence, broken only by the sound of the cars passing on the road out front. And then she heard what she recognized as the waitress's voice as she laughed and said, "No kidding." Sheryl leaned over to peer around the bit of fence. She saw the waitress in her white uniform and the cook in his white pants and T-shirt descend the steps that led from the kitchen. At the bottom, they embraced for a long time, formed in their white clothes one shapeless image in the pale moonlight, then separated and walked in opposite directions toward their cars.

Sheryl listened to both engines as they started, saw both sets of headlights come on. They were gone a good while before she could shake off her sadness and stand. She limped across the lot to the restaurant, climbed the stairs and halfheartedly tried the back door.

Then she sat on the concrete steps. She rested her pocketbook on her lap, folded her arms across it, her elbows in her palms. She leaned against the shingles that covered the cinderblock wall. His bracelet was black in the shade of her arm. She closed her eyes and willed herself to dream of him, but the night grew damp and chilly and her sleep was shallow. Twice she heard the metal clatter of a garbage-can cover, the skitter of tiny feet on the gravel. Even in her half sleep, she was aware of the slow pace of the night and the slow, reluctant way it was lifted.

When she woke for the last time, the air was gray and there was a pale mist through the trees at the edge of the lot, mist draped like ragged bits of cloth over a black line of distant hills.

It was not logical for love to come to nothing, but she must have admitted then, for the first time, that it was certainly possible that it could, like grief, grow forgetful and weary and slowly wear away. She would get older. She would love someone else. She could not live her own life, live through all the coming years of school and friends and marriage and a job, live through the birth of this child she carried, without growing forgetful at times, weary of the pledge she had made. She could not both live and continue to keep them alive.

And yet she could not believe that all her love would come to nothing.

When she began walking that morning, she had only a vague idea of her destination, a vague sense of the challenge she was about to propose. She would choose a public place, but one where only a stroke of luck, a miracle of sorts, would save her.

She would either see him again, refusing all her long life, or she would learn something about the vigilance of the dead.

In the days that followed the fight, he was kept in the jail rooms behind the local police headquarters. It was a new building of orange brick, wide and low, much like a small grammar school, and the police who worked there and dealt mostly with hoods and drunks tended to treat all their guests as incorrigible students with after-school detention. They called Rick Lover Boy and said of him, well within his hearing, "He's seen too many movies."

He spent his days there lying on his cot, breathing through his mouth. His nose had been taped with a wide cross of white adhesive and stuffed with cotton, and his already fuzzy vision (the sunglasses were prescriptive and the police had failed to give him the small horn-rimmed pair his sister brought) was further distorted by the swelling and the pain.

That night, when the arresting officers had brought him to the hospital, the emergency-room nurse had pulled his fingers from his face with a provocative, sexual gentleness, all the while cooing softly, as if to a child. Back in the police station, his father had taken his chin between his thumb and forefinger and examined their work. Even half-blinded, both by the swelling and the station-house lights, Rick could see the way his father drew his lips together and, with his head back, peered at him from under his lids. It was his doctor's face. Rick and his sisters used to imitate it—holding out a thumb at arm's length, squinting at it. "Who am I?" "Daddy!"

His father carefully touched the adhesive and the cardboard splints and then ran his thumb down both sides of Rick's face, lightly and quickly. In the bright station house, it was as close as he could come to a caress, and in the second it provided him to look into his child's face he saw his own wild disbelief, lingering still after more time than should have been needed to accommodate it, that anything he had wanted with such passion could so easily slip through his hands.

Rick turned from his father toward the officers who had brought him in. The father turned from his daughter as she offered him her arm.

In his cell, a small high window let in only a blur of orange sky. There was a parking lot just outside, he knew, then the police garage, then a road and a supermarket. The sounds he heard that first night, an occasional car passing, an occasional car backfiring, burning rubber, were the same sounds he might have heard from his own bedroom at home. But lights were on all through the corridor, and although he could barely distinguish the source from the reflection, he could see the way the light spread itself over the linoleum beside his bed. It was the kind of light he had seen in the hospital, the loony bin, where his mother stayed. He wondered briefly if now he would be just like her.

There were low voices down the corridor. He heard someone say ninety-eight degrees. There were footsteps and a dry hot whisper that was his own breathing.

That night, he dreamed of public places, parking lots and school corridors, the emergency-room nurse leading him by the fingers he could not take from his face. Nothing of Sheryl, nor of the moment when he saw her mother appear behind the screen and knew for certain she was gone. That none of it was true.

The next morning, he asked the attorney they had sent him if he was as much a lawyer as his father was a doctor, but the man only said, "I certainly hope so," unsure whether the chin-out, head-back stance was swagger or mere compensation for the two black eyes. "But you've got yourself quite a little mess."

Rick saw a pink, bald face and a wide white shirt front slashed with a startling string of black. The man said, "First tell me what happened, from the beginning," and as Rick began to speak, reluctantly, and in mumbled half sentences, he felt he had dreamed this too, that he had been in this room, talking like this before.

At one point, the lawyer leaned forward and eyes emerged from what had been two sockets of shadow. And what would he have done, the lawyer asked, his voice puckered with disdain, if she had been there? Elope? Kidnap? Kill her?

Rick shook his head. It occurred to him that he would not be treated this way if he had killed someone.

"Were you planning to hurt her in any way?"

"No," he said. The man waited, seemed to study him. Rick became aware of the labored sound of his own breathing, the dryness of his mouth. It seemed a great advantage to be able to breathe silently, through your nose.

"What, then? Drag her into your car?"

"No." Frowning, insulted, but uncertain if he should say, I wouldn't hurt her, or I'm not that stupid. "It wasn't even my car."

"Threaten her? Scare her?"

He said no again, impatiently, trying to get as much expression of disgust into his eyes as he could. "I just wanted to talk to her."

He heard the man sigh, and his sigh, too, was tainted with dislike. "You drive three cars up onto her lawn," the lawyer said slowly. "You bring all your friends armed with chains, you nearly break her mother's neck, just 'cause you wanted to talk to her? You expect anybody to accept that? You want me to believe that?"

It was the voice, the eyes, the blurred, nearly glossy face of whoever had watched him: that day in the mall, that night in the bowling alley when the bowlers had turned, startled by his cry; the voice, the eyes, of whoever had seen his dream—the baby turned into a pig—who had known the foolish, unaccountable terror it filled him with. Who knew the high feminine sound that escaped from his throat when he made love, who had seen him bare-assed and grinning in the park, coming helplessly at her first touch. The voice, the eyes, the jellied, ill-defined face of whoever watched him, knowing the truth: that he would not escape his life, not even with love.

"Well, I couldn't get her on the phone," he said, and the lawyer put down his pen, ran his fuzzy pink hand down his face and then, holding the thin stripe of his black tie, began to laugh.

Rick bowed his head, breathed a single puff of air through his open mouth and then, closing it, crossing some gulf, slowly, wisely, began to grin.

"So I overreacted," he said.

"Brother," the lawyer said—and hadn't some of the disdain left his voice, weren't they laughing together now, fraternal. "Did you ever."

Rick sat up, held out his hands. There was no doubt in the lawyer's mind what the raised chin was meant to indicate now. The sudden swagger relieved him.

"So what are they going to do to me?" Rick said, as if he were prepared for an easy fistfight. "What are they going to charge me with?"

"Melodrama," the lawyer said. Hoods he could handle. "Making a scene. Stupidity. The whole damn neighborhood saw you."

Rick threw himself back in his chair, the grin giving way to a look of impatient dismissal. Of course she was gone, changed forever. And this was what his life would be like. "I'm sorry," he said in his best sarcastic voice. "I apologize, all right?"

The man smiled, playing his own ace. "Don't apologize to me," he said. "She's the one you got in trouble."

That night or not long after, he woke himself from another nightmare and found that the shame, the sense of embarrassment and profound regret that had broken through his sleep, was no longer at his failure to claim her, to set back the time, but at his attempt.

In the days that followed the fight, a woman pulled into a small gas station somewhere between here and Ohio and asked quickly for the ladies' room. She headed for the back of the station at a run and in her hurry pushed into the door without knocking. She found Sheryl standing at the sink, her wrists held under the running water. She had leaned over and placed her chin on her forearm and at first the woman thought she was about to faint, but she had done it merely to keep his bracelet from the water and the blood.

The woman turned back into the sunlight and called for help. When she turned again, Sheryl was sitting on the floor, her wrists on her thighs, the blood making her black pants shiny and staining the dirty pink tiles. She looked up at the woman somewhat sadly. There was a dark line of blood up the side of her yellow blouse and over her shoulder, made when she had raised her arm to toss back her hair.

The woman took a sheaf of paper towels and nearly covered her with them. Behind her, one of the attendants appeared in the doorway and said, "Jesus Christ."

The small white sink was full of blood. On the ledge between the faucets there was the photograph and a long thin shard of glass.

The woman, who had four children of her own, could not keep the anger from her voice as she wrapped Sheryl's arms in the rough gray towels and asked her over and over, "What were you trying to do?" as if she, or Sheryl, had been somehow mistaken.

At the hospital, someone dialed the phone number Sheryl gave them and found it had been changed. They called the local police station instead. An officer there who had been to that address twice in the past year suggested that a police car would alarm the mother unnecessarily: the girl, after all, and by a sheer stroke of luck, would live. A plainclothes detective, just back from lunch, was asked to do the job instead.

THE SUBURB WHERE WE LIVED, like most, I suppose, was only one in a continuous series of towns and developments that had grown out from the city in the years after the Second World War. They were bedroom communities, incubators, where the neat patterns of the streets, the fenced and leveled yards, the stop signs and traffic lights and soothing repetition of similar homes all helped to convey a sense of order and security and snug predictability. And yet it seems to me now that those of us who lived there then lived nevertheless with a vague and persistent notion, a premonition or memory of possible if not impending doom.

We had among us even then, for instance, families (the Meyers were one of them, I think, and the family that lived behind the Rossis) who had fled here from other, older, suburbs to our east and who spoke to us now like bitter, breathless exiles of what had occurred. Families who assured us that despite their best efforts, their love of the land they had owned there, of the solid brick house that had sat upon it, despite their determination to live out

their lives in the very place where their eldest child had first smiled
and tumbled, the neighborhood—and here they shook their heads,
defeated, resigned—had changed.

We had parents who spoke to us and to each other of the city
streets where they had spent their childhoods as lost forever, wiped
from the face of the earth by change; who said of their old neigh-
borhoods, "You can't go there anymore," as if change had made
a place as inaccessible as a time. Parents who had come from
"what used to be the country," from farmhouses on dirt roads that
we could still see (they told us) were it not for change. Who would
point to a supermarket or a school or a highway overpass and say,
"There, there, that's where it used to be," until it seemed to us that
another world had once existed right beneath our feet, that another world had vanished from the very air we breathed.

We had grandparents, some of us, who remained in embattled
city apartments or dilapidated houses buzzed by highways like flood
victims clinging to chimneys and roofs, caught by the quick and
devastating course of change. We could hear our parents shouting
to them through telephones as if through time, "Mama, when are
you going to get out of there?" "Dad, they want to tear it down!"

Enough, too much, has been said about the cowardly incompe-
tence of memory, how it can be pushed around by time, bullied by
desire, worked over by our intractable ability to see what we want to
see. Even children know you cannot separate the tale from the teller.
And yet it seems to me that even in those snug and orderly days the
word carried a threat that seemed to boil and echo and slowly, inevitably, approach the street where we lived as surely as the sound of
their engines had moved toward us that night.

And it seems to me that, just as we had done with the boys in
their cars, we ignored it. No less than those stubborn and curious
people who build and rebuild their homes on fault lines or slip-

pery mountain slopes or at the edges of ever-eroding rivers and lakes, we seemed to live from day to day either resigned or indifferent to what we knew was coming. We lived from day to day as if the years were circular and the return of a summer or fall just like the last clear evidence that whatever was would last.

Sheryl's father died on the way to work one morning and we shook our heads as if for that family alone things would never again be quite the same.

Just a few years ago, after sodium lights had been placed on the boulevard, giving the present that bright, unreal tinge that more properly belongs to nightmare or memory, and neighbors had begun to gather to form crime patrols (black and white now, although the change that had been spoken of had once meant integration as much as anything else), my parents retired and put their house on the market. I was at the end of my own marriage then, living unhappily in a similar town ten miles away, and when winter came and the house had not yet sold, I agreed to move in so my parents could go south. In the last few years, we had learned a Bible's worth of wisdom regarding muggers and rapists and thieves and one of the tenets of this code was never to let any house, ever, give the appearance of being unoccupied. It was necessary, then, I explained to my fading husband, that I be there whenever a real estate agent brought someone through and that I keep my car in the driveway at night.

I was aware at the time that it was a retreat for me, not so much to the security of my past as away from the awkwardness of my future, but what was cowardly about it was well disguised by what seemed dutiful. My husband nodded as if he believed I would be back. We had by then reached that point in our marriage where we seemed to have lost our capacity for nostalgia, where what we'd shared, that part of our past together that had sustained us until now, had finally worn thin, and only an imagined history, or future, held any promise. We had begun to say we should have moved farther from our parents when we were younger, tried life in another city or state, switched jobs years ago. We should have married later. We said, "Of course, if we'd had children," pretending to be grateful for the freedom our decision, our caution as we had called it, had earned us. If there were children, we could not so easily and amicably part.

I stood at the front door waiting for the real estate woman to arrive. It was February or March, one of those limp, colorless days of late winter. The lawns seemed threadbare, the hedges and trees tangled and pale white. The houses themselves, persistent in their bright colors and definite stripes of aluminum siding, were foolish-looking without an accompaniment of snow or flowers or leaves; they seemed somehow abandoned, washed up on a desolate shore of dry yellow earth and branches the color of driftwood. Across the street, in the driveway of what had been the Rossis' house, the new people had a small boat propped up on cinderblocks and covered with pale green canvas. They had put black bars across their windows—foolishly, we said; things hadn't gotten that bad. Next door, the Carpenters had brown burlap wrapped carefully around each of their small bushes and trees. In Sheryl's old house, the windows were all covered with thick, clear plastic that occasionally caught the dull white sky and then lost it with the next breeze, leaving only black glass.

As the woman pulled into our driveway in her shiny real estate salesman car, I saw that she had the usual couple squeezed into the front seat beside her and some children in the back as well. I took this as a good sign; the ad we'd run in the Sunday paper had been headed, "Bring the Kids!"

The man was the first to emerge and he got out of the car slowly, looking, as they always did, first up at the house and then to his left and right. It was a cold day, but he wore only a short leather jacket with wide lapels and designer blue jeans. There was a handknit muffler cast in various shades of brown and gold at his throat, and he had his fingers in his shallow pockets. He only nodded when I let him in, the real estate woman with her card and her clipboard leading the way, the children still behind them in the car. I put him in his mid-forties at first, but if I count the years more carefully, I would have to believe he was younger than that. He had dark hair and a moustache and pale, somewhat sallow skin. That abrupt, bent, furtive manner of an adult trying not to be shy.

Behind him, his small wife grinned as if she were entering a party where she knew neither the hosts nor the guests nor why she had been invited. She shook my hand when we were introduced and said, "This is nice."

There are, of course, as many different ways for a prospective buyer to look at a house as there are prospective buyers and houses, but I don't think I'd be compromising my belief in the infinitive variety of human potential by saying there are, in general, three or four kinds of lookers. There are the studious ones, who begin in the basement, pace the dimensions of each room, try all the faucets and doors and poke their heads into the attic; the dreamy ones, who walk through each room like well-behaved tourists, noticing what they are told to notice and keeping their hands to themselves; the impatient or embarrassed ones, who seem to need only to confirm that there is, indeed, a house on the inside that more or less conforms to the house on the outside and will gladly take your word for it that there is a basement below and three bedrooms up; and my favorites, those creative, seemingly homeless types who make the imaginative leap to ownership as soon as they walk through the door and spend their entire inspection placing their furniture, setting their table and so thoroughly immersing themselves in their domestic life in this home that they will discuss whether the television in their bedroom will keep the children awake on school nights before they ask how the house is heated or even its price.

Rick, however, when he came through our house that day, was not quite any of these. He followed the real estate agent dutifully, like a dreamer, but then would suddenly break away from her to return to the living room or to reinspect the master bedroom. He asked few questions but answered most of the saleswoman's statistics with "Yeah," or "I know." He neither tapped the walls nor tried the lights nor shoved a screwdriver into the floor joists, but in every room he went first to the windows and carefully, studiously, took in the view. The saleswoman, picking up on this, said a great deal about exposure and sunlight and north winds, but it was clear this did not interest him. Later, in what had been my brother's bedroom, he stood for a good while at the front window, looking out over the driveway and the street, his arms straight at his side.

He was not good-looking. His dark hair was long in the back and poorly cut, his shoulders were narrow and bent. The jacket he wore was cheap, the smell of the leather overcame even the real estate woman's perfume, and he was just heavy enough around the hips to make the pockets of his jeans bulge out a little, showing their white lining. His legs were short, and he wore black socks and scuffed black shoes with silver buckles. He also wore a thin silver wedding ring and there were dark hairs on the back of his thick fingers and hands. Watching him from the hallway just outside the room, where I lingered to answer questions and keep an eye on everything in the house that a prospective buyer might pocket, I thought he seemed like an earnest, ignorant family man who was, would always be, beset and besieged by money problems. Not unlike my own father, I supposed, like all the men who had lived here when I was young.

He turned to me as he again looked around the room. The afternoon light through the windows only emphasized the shadows under his dark eyes. There was a small, pale scar beside his nose, and under his thin moustache one of his front teeth was yellow.

"How long have you lived here?" he asked me.

I said, "Until I was twenty-three."

The saleswoman added, "The house was built in '49."

He looked at her and nodded before meeting her eye.

Across the room, his wife, who was the thorough sort, closed the closet door as if she had made up her mind about something and then announced that she was going out to check on the kids in the car. She had a narrow face and a head of thick frosted hair. Earlier, in the living room, her husband had asked her, "Do you think it's big enough?" and she had slowly raised her eyes to the ceiling, as if the room's dimensions were written on the rafters. "Big enough for what?" she'd said finally, and I recognized the sudden tension between them, the bitterness on her part and on his, the long, weary effort to please.

"For living," he'd answered.

Now he put his hands in his pockets and turned to me again as she left the room. "You ever know Sheryl?" he asked. He motioned toward the window. "She used to live over there."

I nodded. "Sure, I remember her." And then I added, because I hadn't quite made the connection, "Did you know her?"

He pursed his lips just slightly, as if to retard a smile. "Yeah," he said. "I dated her in high school." He said it with a bit of a swagger, and yet coming from a man his age, the expression seemed innocent and quaint. I dated her.

He looked at me carefully, his eyes dark and myopic. "I dated her for over a year," he said.

I smiled, failing to recall for just one moment the details of that night because, for that moment, I was embarrassed for him. He was bragging.

"You do know this neighborhood, then," the real estate woman said. She brushed past me into the hallway. "Great."

He followed her somewhat reluctantly, but then turned. I suppose he was trying to determine how old I was, or would have been then. "Were you a friend?" he asked.

I shook my head. "She was much older," I said. "Or at least then she was older. It wouldn't seem that way now."

The woman had paused in the hallway, the clipboard to her breast. She smiled at me patiently.

"People who seemed much older when you were young have a way of letting you catch up with them," I went on.

She held out her arm to indicate that we should head back downstairs. "Don't they?"

Rick glanced at us both as if we had somehow agreed to thwart him, and then turned to once more lean into the bathroom and reinspect the master, where my parents had slept. Already I had begun to recall the way he had bent, driven his fists into his thighs. Already I had begun to wonder if it could be possible, if he had come back, not merely inadvertently found himself in a place that shocked and surprised him with its significance, but somehow planned, even manipulated this return. Downstairs, I saw him glance at the street again, at what I imagined was her house. I imagined I understood his persistence.

In those days while I waited for the real estate agents to come and lead strangers like judges through our house, empty now of all but the furniture that was to be forever left behind, I found myself recalling again my mother's potions and formulas and earth-bound acrobatics and what they had come to; what Leela's efforts had brought her, and Mrs. Rossi's, what the efforts, the very lives of any of our mothers had finally come to when they looked casually over the heads of their children in the middle of a busy day and saw that even the love that had formed them would not necessarily keep them alive, and yet still I could not quiet the drone of regret that had begun to follow me in those days, the persistent, illogical belief that still, something might have saved us. If there were children, we had said, my husband and I. The very child we had not managed to keep alive. I could not quiet the thud of this old longing not merely to stop time and bring the dead back to life but to discover forever what part of love remains.

As he was about to follow the real estate agent out to the yard, I asked him, "Do you know why she moved away?" There was a coy hint of gossip in my voice that I hadn't intended, a caution, I suppose, against seeming to remember her with too much seriousness.

"The owners?" the real estate agent asked, but Rick turned to me, his hands in his pockets. I suppose I wanted to see him blush, to see tears come into his eyes. Or better yet I wanted him to ask, "No, why?" so I could step into their little drama for the first time, finally deliver the note I'd planned to write. I could imagine putting my hand on the bare bit of wrist that showed above his pocket, under his leather sleeve, behind the ugly, uneven scarf. I could imagine telling him, "There was a child," as if it would prove something. A child as marvelous as any one of us. "Sheryl, I mean," I said.

His hands were in the tight, shallow pockets of his jacket. He didn't move them as he shrugged. "Oh yeah," he said, and what sadness was in his voice was not private, or even personal, but only an acknowledgment of what he knew we all had once shared. "I remember," he said, and nothing more.

When they had made a quick circuit of our yard, the real estate woman climbed the steps to tell me he was interested. "But you'd have to come way down in your price," she said.

I told her I would speak to my parents. When they'd first put the house on the market, my father had been shocked and amazed to discover what it was now worth, and for days and weeks after, he spoke only of what he had paid for the house and what it had come to be valued at, as if they were two halves of an equation that defined the extent of his success. I suppose he was prophetic in this: he died in his sleep, in the coral-colored bedroom I had not yet seen, just two months after the transfer of ownership.

She shook her head. She was an attractive woman with a small, hard mouth, a housewife returned to the marketplace now that her children were gone. She had the impatient air of someone trying to make up for lost time. "Wait on that," she told me. "The wife's not enthused and I've got some people coming by tomorrow who might be better for you. More cash on hand." She checked her clipboard for their name and I looked beyond her to the driveway, where Rick and his wife were leaning against her car. Their children had all gathered to the window at their elbows, were putting their mouths and their noses and the tips of their fingers to the narrow opening in the glass. Through the windshield's yellow reflection I could see someone else was sitting with them, a small, slight old woman with short cropped hair. She seemed to absorb the blows of the children's elbows and feet as if she were lifeless.

The real estate woman named the couple she would be bringing by tomorrow—the couple who would, indeed, prove to be our buyers—and then turned to see what was happening in the back of her car. She waved her hand in the air. "Let's watch the upholstery, dears," she called, and then, to me, "Let me get them out of here."

There was a general opening of the doors as she approached, and the biggest child and her mother got into the front seat beside her. Rick slipped into the back, lifting a smaller one onto his lap. As they pulled out of the drive, he glanced at her house once more. Then his wife twisted in her seat to say something and I saw him press the child's head against his chest as he leaned forward to hear her.

When Billy Rossi died, the front doors all up and down our street remained closed. It was late winter, warm enough to go outside, but the only person I saw on the sidewalk all that long weekend was a reporter for the local paper, who climbed Mr. Carpenter's steps, spoke briefly to him through the door and then, like a contented trick-or-treater, proceeded to Sheryl's old house, where the no longer new owners added, "You couldn't have asked for a nicer kid," to the short potpourri article that appeared the next morning.

We, the neighborhood people, the mothers and fathers and teenage children (there were plenty of us by then), didn't speak together until we met at the funeral parlor, where the carpet and the draperies, the formality of the boy's full name—William Benedict Rossi—on the directory at the entrance and our own Sunday clothes made us all awkward at first, unable to think of anything to say. The coffin was closed, flag-draped. The picture of Billy in his uniform had been taken from the top of the Rossis' television set and propped against the wall.

Mrs. Rossi's black jersey dress would be costume in another year. It had padded shoulders and a wide cinch belt with a rhinestone buckle. She'd had her hair done and wore too much perfume, almost as if she had confused anniversary dinners with this other standard of our social lives. The thick lenses of her black harlequin glasses flashed under the light, but she was not crying. She seemed instead to be dried out, scooped hollow by her grief. I don't think any of us spoke a full sentence to her, or even a complete phrase, but she seemed to forgive us for it. She seemed, in fact, not to expect very much from any of us.

Diane stood beside her in a dark miniskirt and granny glasses, looking sullen and politically well versed, keeping us all from saying whatever inane expression came to mind. Mr. Rossi, as I remember, spent most of the wake on the front porch of the funeral home, talking with his own father, a sprightly old immigrant with dyed hair.

Later, we sat with our fathers in what had somehow been designated as the neighborhood's two rows of folding chairs, while our mothers, who were better at this sort of thing, made a tour of the floral arrangements that lined the walls. They proceeded singly, standing before each arrangement as you might stand before a painting in a gallery, and then, briefly, as if to confirm what they already knew, checking the card. I saw them pause especially before one arrangement, even hesitate so that there was a snag in their progress, a chance for one to motion toward the card and for another, frowning, to lean forward and then whisper, her mouth and eyebrows showing surprise, What do you know?

They returned to us quietly, demurely, although there was something nearly breathless in their manner as they placed themselves in their seats and, almost simultaneously, leaned together. Apparently, they said, Sheryl's mother still had friends or in-laws in town, someone who must have told her about Billy, maybe sent her the article.

We all turned to look at the arrangement Sheryl's mother had sent and then I saw the men cast down their eyes, as if anticipating some compliment.

"Do you remember that night?" my mother was the first one to ask it. "Wasn't that some night?"

The men moved to the edge of their seats as they spoke, and the women turned to one another to nod and shake their heads. Georgie Evers sat just in front of me, and I tapped him on the shoulder and whispered, "Remember how you cried?" I saw the overflow of fleshy neck that capped his shirt collar turn bright red. (Not long after this, and no doubt because of it, he asked me to undress for him. Life, he said, was very short.) Mr. Evers raised his arm to demonstrate a grip he'd used that night. My father lifted his leg and pointed to a spot on his shin. Wasn't that some night, we whispered. Wasn't that some excitement?

"You know, I've seen him around," Mr. Evers said, and his wife added, "Remember how he screamed?"

"Where?" I asked, but she answered, "Out on the front lawn, that night," placing herself, as she had begun to do, between her handsome husband and whoever was young. "I think he was on LSD or something."

"Not then," my father said. "There wasn't LSD then."

"Then they just had beer," my mother said. "And maybe pot."

Mrs. Rossi joined us before I could ask Mr. Evers again, and we fell back into our embarrassed, inarticulate consolations. Finally, my mother mentioned the flowers.

Mrs. Rossi looked toward them. "Yeah, wasn't that nice?" Her voice was thin and careful. "She called me up, too. Last night." She sat down next to me and I had to lean back so the others could hear. "You know what she told me?" she whispered.

The women bent forward, eagerly, I think.

"She told me to move out of my house. That was her advice. She said, Believe me, I've been through it. She said if we didn't, we'd always expect to see Billy, in his bedroom or in the kitchen or something. We'd always be hearing him coming home at night or walking up the stairs." She looked at us through her small, thick lenses. She shrugged and laughed a little. "I don't know where she expects us to go."

"That's silly," Jake's mother said.

(But when we got home that evening, we would all close our front doors, turn on the television before we'd even taken off our coats. We would speak to one another in loud, nearly gay voices, aware that we were thus far free of the kind of longing that would forever haunt the Rossis' house, that persistent, unshakable longing for an irretrievable past.)

"Did she mention Sheryl?" Mrs. Carpenter asked.

Mrs. Rossi touched her beads and held them. We had already begun to look at her differently. That future our parents had set their lives for had come to her as it had once come to Sheryl's mother and her completeness set her apart. "Yes," she said. "She's married. To someone from out there. She's got two kids and a house and all." There was a pause during which the other women, still sitting forward in their seats, seemed to be waiting to be told something more. It was clear that they had hoped or imagined something more for Sheryl: the door flying open and filling the dirty, bloody room with hot sunlight was not miracle enough if it brought her only a life like theirs, two kids and a house and all. Not now, when the poor consequence of that life was so much before them. When the news of whatever she had gained in the time between then and now made them think only of what might be lost.

Mrs. Rossi held out her hands, the large glassy diamond and silver band, a huge blood-red ruby. The gesture seemed to say, Make of it what you will. "I guess everything turned out fine for her after all."

PAM WANTED TO FILL her arms. She thought of flowers and candy, a huge stuffed animal—a giant panda, for instance—or even a potted plant, but in the end merely bundled up her own three children and slid them, protesting, into the cold back seat of the car.

At her parents' house, Sheryl's mother was already waiting by the front door. She frowned when she saw the three children and said, "One of us will have to wait downstairs with them." But Pam walked briskly past her into the hallway and called to her own mother. She bullied her grandmother into shoes and a coat. "We're all going," she announced as she turned the old woman around and tied a muffler at her throat. "I think it's important to have a crowd."

As they'd been doing since Sheryl's return, the three women gave in, believing that Pam, being younger or smarter or just more full of energy than any of them would ever be again, knew best. The grandmother patted her hand and softly murmured something in Polish. Pam shouted at her, "You'll be warm enough?" The old woman nodded, sighing deeply. Pam could smell her sharp breath

and her aunt's sweet perfume and another fragrance that told her
they both had been crying. "You'll be all right?" she asked the
grandmother. The woman continued to nod. On the wall behind
her was the photograph she'd had taken when she'd first arrived in
America. When she'd arrived in Ohio six months ago, she had seen
it as soon as she'd entered the house and, ignoring all the other
portraits of her daughters and her grandchildren and her great-
grandchildren, burst into tears. It took some time before the others
could discover that the word she was crying meant refugee.

"She'll be all right," Sheryl's mother said for her.

Out in the car, Pam told her, "This is the last of it, Ann." (She
had dropped the "Aunt" some time this fall, recognizing her own
new authority.) "Tomorrow we can begin to believe it never happened."

Sheryl's mother nodded. She had rented a house in a nearby
suburb, and Sheryl would begin school there after the winter break.
Her house back east had been sold and the furniture was on its
way. She had found a job in Columbus as a receptionist. Six years
from now she would tell Mrs. Rossi, Leave or you'll always hear
him coming back, because in her sister's house she no longer woke
in the middle of the night believing he was back and beside her.
In the basement family room where she and her mother slept, she
woke only to confirm that the floodlight still shone brightly into
the yard and that her ideas about what to do with her life had not
left her. That she was getting better, getting on.

At the hospital, Pam asked her mother and grandmother to
stay in the car with the children and then took Sheryl's mother's
arm as they crossed the parking lot.

"I'm all right," she said, but Pam held her arm anyway. Tomorrow they might no longer need her.

Sheryl was dressed and sitting in a chair in one corner of the room. The other three beds were empty. Her labor had been long and difficult, but she had gotten through it quietly. The doctor had praised both her courage and her youth. She was wearing one of the plaid maternity blouses Pam had made for her but the change in her body was clear, and although she still held her hands over her stomach, as she had taken to doing during the past few months, her face, suddenly thinner, suddenly seeming to fit properly under the heavy makeup, told them that she was finished with the ordeal.

"I have to ride down in a wheelchair," she said as they entered, and Pam answered—she had been in this hospital herself when her own children were born—"That's standard procedure."

"They don't want you to fall," her mother added.

Sheryl held out her hands to show them she was not carrying anything.

She hadn't wanted to see the child. She'd told them there was no point in it. But Pam was persistent, certain it was this, the children she had held in her arms, that carried her into her own future when the chasm at the heart of her daily life drained her of hope. She asked a nurse she remembered to give the girl another chance.

Sheryl had just finished her first breakfast when the nurse walked halfway into the room. "Just a peek?" she asked.

Sheryl merely nodded.

The thing was incredibly small and ugly and would not open its eyes. Sheryl unwrapped it and touched its elbows and knees, the waxy remnant of its cord. His skin was pale and tinged with yellow and his fingers were tightly closed. She pressed her lips to the top of his head, brushed them against the fine dark hair, touched the eyelids and lips in a kind of blessing. Then she closed up the blanket and handed the child back to the nurse. The first and last time she would see him.

They brought the wheelchair to the door of the room, and

Sheryl stood slowly, her cousin and her mother at her elbow. "I'm all right," she told them.

Out in the corridor, other women in nightgowns and slippers, blue or pink ribbons in their hair, walked slowly up and down, touching the walls. They looked carefully at Sheryl, only a small suitcase in her lap. She was wheeled the long way around to the elevators, avoiding the nursery.

Pam ran ahead to pull the car up to the hospital's entrance. Sheryl and her mother and the orderly who pushed her waited together in silence. She was surprised to see her aunt and her grandmother and the three children in the car. She could tell already that her grandmother had tears in her eyes.

There was a great fuss about who would sit where, and Pam swept all the children out of the car as if she were rearranging the luggage in a small trunk. She sent two of them around to the other side as the grandmother moved into the middle and then, as Sheryl got in, lifted the youngest child into her lap. "You don't mind," she said. "Watch your fingers," and shut the door.

Sheryl's mother and aunt rode in the front seat beside Pam. Her grandmother's fleshy elbow pushed into her side. The child squirmed on her lap. Outside, the streets they passed were dull with winter, the lawns gray, and the remaining Christmas decorations, strings of lights and plastic Santas and Nativity scenes littered with scraps of snow seemed, as they always seemed in those days after Christmas, colorless and limp. Next year they'd look new again.

Her little cousin felt the tag on her wrist and began to finger it. Next year she'd be in her new house and her new school. The child—traveling now in another car, in the arms of a woman who, Pam had told her, had nearly given up hope—would be nearing its first birthday.

She bowed her head and put her lips to her cousin's fine hair.

Sheryl shrugs and pulls herself from the chair. She climbs the stairs slowly, her hand trailing along the banister.

The lights of her vanity mirror seem dim in the red evening sunshine that fills her room. She sits before it, carefully studies her face, then reaches for the thick blue compact. With one hand steadying the wrist of the other, she draws a careful black line across each eyelid. She lifts a hank of hair, rats it vigorously, wets it with hairspray. Her lipstick tastes of peppermint although no one has yet to share the flavor. She slips a thick plastic bracelet over her wrist, and then another. The sound of them, she knows, will reach the boys, make them turn away from their cars. She practices a slow, wise smile.

She wants to love someone else. This emptiness left like an impression by the way she loved her father must be filled or else it will be as though he never lived.

Downstairs, her mother and grandmother are watching an unfamiliar program on TV, thrust a half an hour too early into their evening because there were so few dishes to be done. Her grandmother clucks her tongue when she sees her tight clothes. Her mother says only, "Nine o'clock," no kindness in her voice now, only the sense that she had once thought her children would save her but there is no relief.

She leaves by the front door, going quickly down the three steps and across the lawn. Jake stops on his bicycle to watch her. My parents peer over the rhododendron. Mrs. Evers, eyeing her carefully, knowing what she is dressed for, says "Hi" as she brings her garbage to the curb.

The air is still hot and her shoes echo against the pavement. There is the pale swish of lawn sprinklers, children appearing here and there, in trees, behind fences, across the grass, as numerous as fireflies.

The woman who had nearly given up hope, Pam had told her, would be pushed from the hospital in a wheelchair, the baby in her arms, just to make the picture complete.

Sheryl brushed her lips against her cousin's hair, his determined squirming like an echo of the child she had carried. What she thought of then was not the nights they had shared, or of all that had insinuated itself between them since the door flew open and her life began again. What she thought of instead was summer. Another summer evening on our street. The dinnertime stillness slowly giving way, the sound of chairs scraping away from tables and, through window screens and opened doors, of dishes tumbling in sinks full of water. Children, numbed briefly with food and already taller than they had been, stepping out into the new light, walking carefully into the cooled air, across the lengthening shadows. Her father's death still new to her; her throat still strained with the effort of not calling out his name.

The three females linger at the table. The plates before them are full of food, only the crumpled paper napkins and the empty glasses and the silverware crossed over each plate mark the time that has passed since they sat down. Her grandmother says, "Too hot to eat," although there is only cold meat and salad. Her mother wipes her throat with a napkin. "There was a breeze," looking toward the dining room ceiling, into the still air, "but it's gone." Her voice saying of course. Of course there is no relief.

Sheryl moves her bare thighs, pulling them from the sticky plastic seat. "Can I go?" she asks, and her mother nods and tells her somewhat indifferently to be home by nine. Then something in her face seems to relent.

"There's a movie on TV tonight," she offers in a way that implies she is doing her best, but it's hard enough keeping herself alive. "When the ice-cream man comes, I'll pick up some ices."

Angie is waiting for her at the corner. Sheryl greets her with a piece of gum and the two girls turn, their hips bumping and their shoes scraping over the sidewalk, and once more head for the school-yard, where they know the boys will be.

The miracle, then, was not the door banging open and filling the small bloody room with hot sunlight, bringing her more life; the miracle was that, despite all she had lost, despite all she knew was no longer true—her love alone was not enough, it would always, eventually, come to nothing—still, there was the blind, insistent longing, stirred now by the child in her arms, that this emptiness be filled again.

In the front seat, Pam, her mother and her aunt were keeping up a bright conversation to which the three children added their own bright and nonsensical things. Sheryl pulled her small cousin closer to her, held him more tightly in her arms. She tossed her hair back over her shoulder as Pam drove out onto the highway and the car picked up speed.